PROPOSING BLISS

A BLISS SERIES NOVELLA

MICHELLE JO QUINN

ISBN: 978-0-9951506-2-1

Print ISBN: 978-0-9951506-3-8

To Joe,
with all my heart.

ACKNOWLEDGMENTS

It takes a modern village to write a book.
I couldn't have done it without Dayna's magic and
Elizabeth's keen eye on details.

To Lucy Rhodes, I say again, you make beautiful covers!

I'm grateful for my family and their overflowing
support.

To the writing community, writer friends: Trinity, Amie,
Liz, Amanda, Gaby, Talia and many more, stay awesome.
Your friendship means the world to me.

To friends Cathy, Aline and Brenda, you're all amazing!

To my children, Ethan and Violet, I love you both.

To my husband, Joe, you're cool. I think I'll keep you!

UNE AFFAIRE AU RETENIR

LEVI

Two years ago...

The night began like any other night—with me bored out of my head. I shook hands with the right people, talked business with others, and kissed a few too many women—who replied with subtle and some not-so-subtle gropes. In a black, tailored tuxedo, I stood beside my date for the gala, Louisa Marie Alfonso-Parker. Though her divorce wouldn't be final for another week, she thought she should make a new start, soon. And she had targeted me for trial-and-error purposes. By the way the night was going, I was leaning more toward error.

Throughout the night, I kept wondering what in the world had possessed me to accept her invitation. She was gorgeous, but her personality was drier than the Gobi desert. No amount of single malt could drown her mind-numbing political tirade.

My phone buzzed in my pocket, and I fished it out, hoping it was a means of escape. As I viewed the name on my screen, I was reminded that there were worse people out there than my date *du jour*.

"Olivier, must you work all the time? It's time to play, dahlin'," Louisa said through gritted teeth, and her nails skimmed the side of my neck.

I cringed, removing her claws before she drew blood. She hated not having anyone's full attention. "I won't be long," I told her, and ignored the plumes of dark smoke coming out of her ears.

The phone call I was about to take was rather... delicate, or indelicate depending on the other person. I didn't need an audience. Dodging the attendees in varied black-and-white attire, I made my way to one corner of the grand ballroom before answering the call.

"Ophelia?" I kept my voice flat. No need to excite her.

"Hello, lover," she drawled.

The wannabe actress/model had been a huge pain in my derrière ever since I'd made the mistake of taking her on a date. It had been a dare.

Huffing out a breath, I looked up to the gilded ceilings. "I thought I asked you not to call me again." *Many times over.*

"Oh, but you weren't serious." I could practically hear her silicon-plumped lips pouting. "When are you coming home? I'm cold and lonely."

"I made it clear that I didn't want to see you anymore, remember? Remember when you keyed my new car?" Just the thought of what she had done to my

Tesla made my blood pressure rise to dangerous levels. "I won't file charges, but you promised not to come near me again." Calm, I had to stay calm.

A sharp intake of breath came through the line before a maniacal laugh pierced my ear.

"You were just playing hard to get." She purred and moaned. "Check your phone. I sent you a selfie that will make you want me back." I didn't trust the confidence in her voice.

A ping sounded from my phone. I pulled it away from my ear to see what she had sent me. I shouldn't have, but I was glad I did. For there she was. All of her cosmetically-altered, naked self was spread-eagle on *my* cloud-grey sateen sheets. The ones on my bed, in my master bedroom, which Ophelia shouldn't have access to. As soon as I ended the call, I needed to reconsider acquiring a restraining order.

"How did you get into my penthouse?" I yelled at the phone, garnering stares and unwanted attention from people around me.

"I have my ways." Her voice took on a salacious tone. "So are you coming back soon?"

I *had* been patient for far too long. "All right, Ophelia, stay put. Do not move." I enunciated those last three words. Before she could say anything else, I disconnected and tapped in another number. "Jerrod, explain to me how someone was able to enter my apartment. The same woman who vandalized my car yesterday."

The head of security of my building stuttered an incoherent response. Not many had witnessed or experienced an angry Laurent. Jerrod went right into action, not making any excuses. He promised to handle my intruder personally and, if the authorities had to be contacted, that I would receive immediate reports. I then called my lawyer for the R.O. and had him get in touch with Blackwood Security for a more reliable and current system for my penthouse.

I had just ended that last call when, through the doors I stood next to, came a woman in a simple black dress, ass first. *Delightful.* Facing away from me, she leaned over a rolling tray, pulling it out from the kitchen. Staring right at that tempting behind, I didn't move fast enough. Her buttocks bumped me right where they should, but her right heel pierced my foot.

Alerted, electrified, and high on the buzz, I grabbed her hips just as she turned.

"Oh my goodness! I'm so sorry!" She pressed a hand on her chest.

She was a goddess.

Everything slowed down. All I could hear was the swift tattoo of my heart. The rest of the world disappeared into a puff of smoke. No one else was present except her and me.

The neckline of her 50's-style dress displayed a décolletage waiting to be explored. A string of pearls wrapped delicately around a neck that was aching to be kissed. The smooth skin of her jaw begged me for a nibble. And when my eyes met hers, cliché as it might sound, I felt that I had died and gone to heaven. My mind was a dense fog, but the sight of her was clear as day, as illuminating as the sun, as bright as the stars. *Be still, my beating heart.*

"You can let go of me now." Her voice somehow broke through. I gazed at her again, from her crown of caramel braids down to pink toes peeking out of her black, unadorned shoes. "Let go...please."

I followed the resonance of her voice—as though I could see it—from the edge of her neckline, up to her elegant throat and to heart-shaped, pursed lips. Then, one by one, she extracted my fingers from her hips, and daintily plucked the top of her dress and righted it.

"You can stop staring at my cleavage," the goddess admonished me. My eyes dropped to my hands, to the electrified parts of my skin she had touched.

When I looked up again, I stepped back from the disdain and clear disgust on her face. She might as well have called me 'pervert'. Possibly remembering where we were, her pursed lips and furrowed forehead melted into a slightly more serene countenance.

Any other time, I would have thought she had a screw loose, managing to go from one emotion to the next in one second flat. But I'd dealt with my fair share of crazies, and there wasn't any doubt in my mind that she wasn't one. She was pure and simple and beautiful.

And I had to know her.

But the first words that came out of my mouth weren't entirely what I had in mind. "There wasn't much to see." I was an idiot. What I'd meant to say was that I wasn't staring at her breasts.

Before I could rephrase my words, she "humphed!"

her way around and back to the task at hand, angling the cart toward the main bar. As she stepped away, she muttered, "Should have stepped on your other foot too."

A quiet laugh escaped my mouth. It was something I hadn't done in a while, and it sounded strange. All I could do was watch the swing of her glorious hips as she moved forward, fast.

I muttered out loud this time, "Be still, my beating heart," and placed a hand over the erratic tattoo in my chest.

"Levi!"

I had trouble turning away from the goddess and toward the source of the voice which had called me. A man in his late sixties with an antalgic gait waved as he ambled up to me. His heaving paunch pushed the limits of the buttons on his shirt.

"Santiago, how are you doing?" Still reeling from the excitement of bumping against the sweet-looking woman, I shook his hand with gusto.

He returned my greeting with a big smile on his face. "Very well, son. Still surviving. How's your dear grandmother doing?"

"Martina was doing great last time I spoke to her."

Santiago leaned closer and jabbed my side with his plump arm. "It's okay, son, you can tell me that she's angry as the devil himself. How did her grapes survive the early frost?"

I shook my head and raised my hands in front of me. "You've known her far longer than I have, Santiago. You know how she gets." As tender and loving my grandmother was with me, she was a wrathful demoness when things didn't go her way. She had a love-hate relationship with Mother Nature, and oftentimes she would be found sleeping beside The Farmer's Almanac. "I've read reviews for your wine. Congratulations! Now that you've reached the top, isn't it about time to retire?"

The older man guffawed and coughed, clasping and adjusting his collar. "Never! I will be harvesting those grapes until my last breath. Now, tell me, son: Martina has taught you all her secrets. Isn't it time you branch out on your own? Run your own vineyard?"

I scratched the back of my neck. "Not in the stars, Santiago, not for me. It's best for people who have the heart to get shit done, who don't mind all the work and dirt on their hands."

"I wouldn't blame you." Santiago ducked his head and peered around us, waving a hand in the air. "Who in their right mind would give up waking whenever you want, with any woman you want, and only getting up to party all over again, eh?"

"Who indeed?" It was hard to explain, but there was a sudden emptiness inside as I said those words. I glanced to my left, and almost too easily, my eyes found *her* again, talking amicably with one of the bartenders.

What would be her views on this matter? On someone like me? I wondered, while I watched her from afar, the goddess with the sweet smile who had captured my heart.

THROUGHOUT THE NIGHT, I tried in vain to find out who she was. No one seemed to know her, or even cared to figure it out. She was like a ghost haunting the ballroom, flying from one corner of the expansive hall to the next with little effort. After a while, I accepted that most, if not all, the event's attendees were rich, self-centered bores.

During dinner Louisa asked me to take a seat next to hers, and there I sat, but my mind roamed and my eyes darted from one area to the next. After desserts, I spotted her talking to Evelyn Witham, the chairwoman of the charity for which the fundraising gala was held.

There it was, another chance to figure out who the mystery woman was. Could I redeem myself? "Louisa, there's Evelyn." I nodded my head slightly in their direction. "Do you know who's talking to her?" I hoped that my voice did not betray me.

"Hmmm...I've never seen her before." Louisa pursed her lips, which reminded me of an anteater.

How could everyone else not notice her? "She's been here all night."

Louisa extended her neck and leered at me. "Maybe she's the help." She said the last word like it was a curse. "Viola would know. Viola," she called across the table, and Viola duBarry did not hesitate to appear interested. "Do you know who that girl is talking to Evelyn?"

"I think she's the event planner," the woman replied.

I bit the inside of my lip to stop myself from asking more questions, from appearing too eager.

"Planner? I thought Jayleen did this? Did they fire

her? I just saw her at the club last week, and she'd been going on about this whole night," Louisa pressed.

Viola flattened a hand on her chest and leaned forward, but did not lower her voice. Meekness was lost to some of these women. "That's what I heard. Apparently, Evelyn found out Jayleen took some of the funds for personal purposes. Jayleen does have a new convertible."

Louisa quirked her eyebrow, while I remained, with bated breath, waiting for these two women to confirm whether my goddess was indeed the planner.

"Where did they find this one?" Louisa flicked a finger over her shoulder, like a fly had been annoying her. "I've never seen her in the circle before. She can't be new. Why would they get someone new to replace a veteran?"

"Maybe they wanted someone with fresh ideas," I put in, careful not to inflect my tone and betray my true emotions.

Louisa turned to me and scoffed. "Have you not seen what Jayleen can do? She planned my wedding!"

"And that's a great example? You're getting divorced after six months of marriage." I was preparing my own grave if I didn't stop mocking Louisa.

"Apparently, Evelyn worked with her in some art gallery opening, or something a couple months back," Viola added.

Louisa turned her head again, wrinkled her nose and said, "Look at her. She can't even afford a proper couture gown for tonight. You can practically smell the mothballs from here."

That was enough to tip me over. "I'm surprised you even knew what mothballs are, Louisa." I stood abruptly and straightened my suit jacket. "I thought the only balls you knew were your ex-husband's old, hairy ones." I strutted away from the table as I heard a collective gasp.

Once I was a few feet away from the goddess and Evelyn, my heart thumped like a high school drum line in my chest. I couldn't count each beat, and I tried—and failed—to steady my breathing, lest I sounded like I had run a marathon when I reached them. I knew she sensed me. Within a quarter of a beat, our eyes met, my line of vision blurred, I grinned like a fool, and my step faltered. She did not return my smile.

Whether she had heard of me, recognized me, or just understood the type of person I was in a matter of seconds, she didn't like me, and it showed. Her head nodded once, and a small smile played on her pink lips as she turned her attention back to Evelyn, before hastily leaving her side.

I was a mountain of patience, and I welcomed challenges.

"Evie," I called.

"Levi, you're looking rather dashing tonight." She placed a hand to my cheek as she welcomed a swift kiss on hers.

"Just tonight?"

She laughed.

"Who was that you were just talking to?" I was tired of skirting around the issue.

Evelyn laughed again. "I can always depend on you

to keep me entertained. She's none of your business, my dear boy." Evelyn Richland reminded me of my grandmother. Beautiful, even at her age, and like Martina, she had a pure heart.

I offered a charming grin. "C'mon, Evie, all I need is a name."

"Levi," she began, holding my hands in hers, and staring me straight in the eye, "She is the type of girl who believes in romance, in being swept away, not only by charm and dashing good looks—" She waved a hand at me. "—but by true love. She is a girl who believes in happily ever after, and Levi…Veronica deserves it."

Veronica. My throat constricted at the mention of her name. "I believe in all that too." Not until I said the words did I understand what they meant and that I, in fact, was honest saying them. There was a heaviness in my chest, like I had been punched in my solar plexus, which knocked the air out of my lungs until I could find a way to recover. I pulled at the bow tie around my collar, ensuring that it hadn't tightened.

"Dear Levi, you may think you do, but it hasn't seemed that way for years. I've watched you with other women. I've seen how you are, heard of what you've done to them. Best to stay away from Veronica. A girl like her deserves to be loved purely and honestly."

Evelyn was an intelligent woman, capable of growing her own empire with her head high and her integrity intact, much like Martina. I had had the privilege of acquiring her wisdom through the years, and it would be wise for me to listen to her now. But my heart was a stubborn machine, and I was a stubborn man.

"Levi, dahling, there you are!" Louisa's hand snaked over my arm and up my shoulder, digging her nails in. "Hello, Evelyn, another lovely event as usual."

"Louisa, I see you've moved on without thinking, once again."

The two women threw words at each other. Meanwhile, my heart began its fast tattoo once more, and it told me one thing: Veronica was nearby. I watched her cross the room weaving through a sea of people. I held my breath as she collided with a man. His drink spilled all over the front of her dress, and his hand stroked too aggressively over her chest. My hands fisted at my sides, and I was ready to grab his grubby hands away from Veronica.

One of the bartenders interfered and handed Veronica a cloth, while turning the man away. Two other staff approached and guided the man, who was clearly inebriated, out of the ballroom. She and the bartender surreptitiously exited the ballroom through one of the side doors, which led to the terrace.

"Excuse me, I have something..." I didn't finish what I wanted to say. I yanked my hand away from Louisa's grasp and ignored her calling my name.

I had to find her, to check and see that she was okay. The crowd had moved toward the middle of the room where the dance floor had been set up. Taking a different door on the side, I slipped out into the cool night. The threat of rain hung in the air.

"What an ass!" The deep timbre of a man's voice boomed. "Your dress is never going to be the same, Nica."

Nica? Was that a shortened version of Veronica? I preferred her full name. I moved closer, hiding behind a topiary. The pulse in my neck thumped madly.

"I know. And it's my favorite, too. Are you sure I can't have it dry-cleaned?" I remembered the sweet tone of her voice from earlier. This time, there was a hint of sadness in it. I wanted to walk over there and kiss the frown away.

"No, hon, 'fraid not. You can try to hand wash it but be very, very careful. It's real vintage."

Her laughter suspended in the air like sleigh bells on a wintry night. I committed it to memory. One day, I would elicit those sweet giggles from her, among other sounds.

"Real vintage? Is there such a thing?" she asked.

"You know what I mean. Well, I'd better get in there before Pyotr gets wild with the vodka. You coming in?"

"I will in a few. I just need to breathe for a bit."

Through the spaces between the leaves, I saw the tall bartender wrap Veronica in his arms. "We're so proud of you. Last-minute, and you came up with this amazing event." He kissed the top of her head. How I ached to do that.

"Thanks, Gerard. Seriously, thanks for tonight. I couldn't have done it without you guys. I'll be back in, straight to the kitchen. I wanna raid those unserved desserts."

As I pressed against the plant, the leaves rustled. The bartender and Veronica looked up. I cursed at myself. And when the man, Gerard, said, "I think you should come in now. It's not safe here. There might be *perverts* in the bushes," I cursed myself again.

Veronica took his advice, tilting her head to the side to check on the intrusion. Me. They walked back into the ballroom, leaving me cold and angry at myself for losing that first chance of alone time with her.

And it was my last and only chance that night.

When I returned to the gala, a hand gripped my arm. Cynthia Benjamin greeted me with a wide smile on her face. She was as close to an aunt as I could ever have. "Cynthia!" I kissed both her cheeks.

"I didn't know you were going to be here. Who was the lucky lady?" Cynthia asked, flattening the lapels of my jacket.

"I was *unlucky* enough to say yes to Louisa Marie Alfonso-Parker." Cynthia hissed. "Yes, I know, I know. It was better than the alternative."

"Which was?"

I wasn't ready to admit that I'd accepted because I didn't want to be alone. Misery sure loved company. "I'm not entirely sure. You're a bit late to the party."

"Fashionably late, my dear. We had some issues with Isobel. I swear that girl will be the death of me." She rubbed her temples, trying to ease thoughts of her rebellious teen daughter.

"You just think that because your firstborn is near perfect. Speaking of whom, has he told you?"

"Yes—" She clapped her hands together. "—and we can't be happier. I'm glad the decision came from him. Although I have a feeling I have you to thank as well." She patted my chest.

"It was all Jake's idea." It had been. My best friend, after several years of being the fascinating, talented doctor he was in some other part of the world, had decided to return to California to be closer to his family. "Build roots," he had said, "fall in love. Start a family." Just two nights ago, while on the phone with him, I'd thought he'd lost his mind. I thought he'd contracted dengue fever and had been completely delusional. Jake and I had approached life like a game, always competing to see who would end on top, even when it came to women.

Two days ago, he'd confessed that he'd been exhausted and lonely, and searching for a real purpose, for true happiness. Despite his love for what he'd been doing, something was missing from his life. It was time for him to grow up, and he had advised me to do the same. I'd laughed at him but regretted not telling him that I had been feeling quite lost as well.

Until tonight.

"We're so proud of him." Cynthia's words brought me back from my recollections.

"As am I." And that hit me harder than a brick wall. I immediately zeroed in on Veronica, huddled behind the bar, sneaking a bite of something into her mouth.

Evelyn had advised me to stay clear of Veronica, because I wasn't the right man for her. I could be. I could turn myself into someone Veronica would be proud to call hers. It didn't matter that her vintage dress was old; she cherished it, which meant she wasn't enamored by glitz and glamour. I'd witnessed enough men—wealthy, good-looking, of different pedigrees—

approach her throughout the night, and all she did was politely smile at them and walk away.

She wanted romance.

She wanted happily ever after.

She wanted true love.

I could be the man to sweep her off her feet. And I knew how to start.

After excusing myself from Cynthia, I searched for Santiago.

Before the event ended, I walked out of the grand ballroom without Louisa's arm wrapped around mine, with my own new venture, and my thoughts filled with a goddess in a black vintage dress, Veronica—the woman who would turn my life around.

BLISS BEFORE THE STORM

VERONICA

Many moons later...

*H*ow could I ask him to go, while at the same time ask him *not* to go? Maybe I could figure it out later, when he looked less sexy.

I blew a raspberry that fanned the hair on my forehead.

Like that was ever going to happen. Levi, less sexy? Never with a capital 'N'!

Not when he had on black Armani boxer briefs that left little to the imagination, his glasses, and nothing else. Problem was, I didn't have to imagine. I could pull those down, past the tattoo on his hip, and take a nice, long peek at his...

"Did you say something?"

Eyes up! "What?" I propped my elbows on the mattress.

Levi peered over his glasses. He'd totally caught me, red-handed and dirty-minded! I cleared my throat and dragged my eyes back to what I was reading: some hoity-toity Sweet Sixteen event details.

Levi snapped his book closed and set it aside. He reached for me, ghosting the pads of his fingers along my spine, pushing my shirt up and off. Then he blew warm breath from the small of my back all the way to the nape of my neck.

I was drowning in desire. How could I work with him around?

"You wanted to ask me something, sweetheart?"

"Hmmmm..." Closing my eyes, I hummed at the vibration of his voice behind my ear. "I didn't say anything."

"Oh, but you have that look."

"What look?" A look of want? Of fire-coated desire? I screwed my eyes tighter when he pushed my bra strap off one shoulder and peppered kisses on my skin.

"All you have to do is ask me, my sweet, sweet love." He punctuated those words with flicks of his tongue along my neck.

"I didn't say... I... Levi, you gotta stop or I... Please let me finish." I panted in between words, while Levi trailed those kisses down my back to one side of my ribs.

Then he stopped. Completely. And leaned away from me.

Looking over my shoulder, I gaped at him. He sat against the headboard, grinning. "Why did you stop?" I protested.

He shrugged and cocked his head to one side. "You told me to."

I pouted. Reaching forward, Levi tilted my chin up, tugged my bottom lip and leaned in for a quick kiss.

"Now, ask me." He sat back, arms crossed over his chest, and had that sexy smirk on his face.

"I don't know what you're talking about." Trying to ignore him, I glared at the paperwork before me.

"Veronica, you are a horrible liar." Levi added a chuckle. He wrapped his arms around my waist and propped his chin on my shoulder.

I clicked my tongue, feeling like I'd already lost this battle and I might as well give up. "What makes you think I'm lying?"

"For one, you can't even look at me." I stared at him over my shoulder and then narrowed my eyes to prove a point. Yet, he continued. "And...your mother called me today."

I disengaged from him, turned to face him and sat on my heels. My head swam from my quick change of position, but I shook it off. "She what?" My voice raised an octave higher.

"Relax, love, she asked me if I'm going home for Thanksgiving with you."

That sneaky little she-devil! No wonder she'd bugged me with so many questions about Thanksgiving dinner this weekend.

"She thought it was time to meet the man *schtupping* her daughter. Those were her exact words, by the way." Levi's shoulders shook with laughter.

I huffed. It was so like my mother to go behind my

back like this. Time for plan B. Ducking my head, I flipped innocently through the pages of work beside me. "You don't have to come. It's just a boring dinner with my mother and my sister. Nothing huge. Maggie might not even be there. For the last two years she's gone to her boyfriend's for the Holidays."

"Oh, but she said everyone will be there this year, and they're all eager to meet me." *Damnit Mother!*

I crawled seductively to him, batting my lashes and licking my lips, and straddled his lap. "Or..." I trailed a finger from the hollow of his throat down to the center of his deliciously toned abs. "We can just forget all about it and stay here all...weekend...long, without any disruptions." I peered up at him from under my lashes, caught my bottom lip between my teeth and let my finger wander further south.

His attention panned to that last bit. I let go of my lip and licked the center of his slightly parted lips. He moaned and tickled my sides. I bucked on top of him.

"Nice try, you little nymph. We're going. Unless you're too embarrassed to introduce me to your family?"

"Embarrassed? No, not at all. I'd love for you to meet them one day...someday—" *Never.* "—It's just..."

Worry filled his blue eyes.

"My mother isn't the best cook. We might end up eating sandwiches...which, for her, is still a stretch."

His expression changed into something more relaxed. "I'm sure it'll be fine. I told her I'll bring wine. I'll bring a case so we can gargle with it if the food is thoroughly inedible."

He didn't know how likely it was that would happen. Clearly, he'd thought about this and determined it was a great idea. It was impossible to win when he'd already made up his mind. "Okay, fine, you can come."

"I love it when you say that." Levi nuzzled my neck, pushing my hair off to the side.

"Pervert." I playfully slapped his naked chest and tilted my head so he could access more sensitive areas.

"What are you bringing?" he asked against the apex of my shoulder and neck.

Now, that was the million-dollar question. Levi still had no idea of my lack of cooking skills. I mean zero. Nada. Zilch. I could eat food, I could serve it, but I could not cook it.

"What I bring every year, Rice Krispie squares with Reese's Pieces."

He stopped nibbling on my earlobe and looked at me straight on. "What are those?"

I chuckled. "What do you mean what are those? What do you think?" He shrugged. Oh my god. "You don't know what Rice Krispie squares are! Oh you poor, rich, sheltered man."

"I could take a wild guess that they're made out of rice."

"Not rice, rice cereal. And butter and marshmallows. They're super good. I pretty much grew up eating them." Wrong! I grew up eating those and only those. "I'll make extra to keep here for snacks."

"All right. Sounds delish. Speaking of snacks..." His fingers made their way up my back, and underneath my bra clasp. I swatted at his arms. "No. I have work to do.

21

Go read your book." I reached for my paperwork. He took it from me and threw it on the floor. I gasped. I would have protested louder, but Levi showed me some other more pressing matters.

L'ACTION DE GRACE

LEVI

To say Veronica was nervous would be an understatement. I reached over and grabbed her hands to stop her from wringing them. I was afraid that she would separate her joints in frustration. I'd had a hard enough time getting her into the car. She'd tried to come up with unbelievable excuses just so I would give up and tell her that we could stay.

Her last attempt had nearly worked. When she told me she hadn't worn underwear, I'd been tempted, but once I devastatingly discovered that she'd fibbed, the plan was back on.

"Why are you so anxious? It's just me. I love you no matter what happens tonight." I glanced away from the road to give her a once-over.

Her shoulders slouched forward as she sighed. "I wish it was just that. It's not you that's the problem. And it's not Maggie. You'll take a liking to her for sure."

She paused and worked her bottom lip between her teeth. "It's my mother."

I chuckled. Maybe I shouldn't have. Her mother couldn't be as intolerable as mine. "She sounded lovely over the phone."

"Ha! Right. Because it wasn't freaky enough that she managed to track you down and force you to come for Thanksgiving dinner." I kept my eyes on the road, but I could feel the tension emanating from her as she spoke. "Don't you find that a little bit odd? I asked her how she did it and she said 'I have my ways, Nica'. I mean, come on!" Her hands detached from mine and flew in the air.

"I thought it was sweet. I would have met her eventually." I placated her, taking one of her hands again and bringing it to my lips. "Veronica, I'm very serious about this relationship. I would have asked to meet your family sooner or later." *Just as long as she didn't ask to meet mine.*

She huffed out a heavy breath. "Fine. But you can't say that I didn't warn you. And you can't blame me for anything wrong that happens. Ever."

"I promise." I kissed her hand again and snickered against it. Looking over, I saw her pout and could not help but be a tad nervous myself. I was great with families and parents when I wasn't too serious about the relationship. But with Veronica...I'd suffer if something happened to us.

This had to work. I had to impress her family, let them know I was the right man for Veronica, even though, through and through, I hated to admit I wasn't worthy of her love.

As soon as we parked on the driveway of her childhood home, a portly woman dressed in a plum taffeta evening dress waved at us from the porch. I kept my laughter in check as I unfolded myself out of the car, walked to the back, and opened the trunk.

"Oh my freaking lord." Veronica groaned beside me, gripping me like she had talons. Her face paled. "What is she wearing?"

"Hallooooo!" Her mother glided down the steps to us, patting her hair in place as she approached. She practically pushed her daughter aside to get to me, and when she did, she hugged me so tight I struggled to catch my breath.

Veronica's eyes widened. She swung herself toward her mother and tried to peel her away from me. "Mom, you're choking him!"

I straightened as soon as she let me breathe. God, for someone a head and a half shorter than me, the woman was strong.

She placed a hand over her chest. "Oops, sorry. I get a little bit excited sometimes."

"Not to worry. I'm still in one piece." Before I could retract that last statement, worried that I had offended her, she cackled.

She turned to her daughter. "Oh, I like this one, Nica, he's funny. And so handsome too!" She pinched my left cheek.

"Oh my god," I heard Veronica say again. Panic replaced her embarrassment. "Maggie! Help me out here!"

A tall girl with curly blonde hair came bounding

down the steps and swung an arm over their mother. "Can't you wait 'til they get in the house at least? Hi, I'm Maggie, and you're Levi." She extended a hand.

"Pleasure."

"Come bring your stuff inside." Maggie nodded toward the house, a small yellow Cape Cod with an expansive and well-cared-for garden in the front.

"We don't have stuff. We only brought Rice Krispie treats and wine. They're in the car," Veronica told them.

"Well...not exactly." I was going to pay for this. I gave Veronica a crooked smile while I took a bag out of my trunk. "We're staying for the weekend."

Veronica gaped.

"Your Mum made me promise to keep it a secret." The look Veronica gave me said enough. If I was the type to shake in my boots, I would have.

Maggie whistled. "Oh boy, you're in deep shit now." She clapped my shoulder and shook her head. "Bad move, Levi, bad move. And here I thought you looked smart. I guess pretty doesn't always come with brains, even for guys."

Veronica huffed and turned on her heels. She stomped all the way to the open light blue door.

"Oh, don't you worry about her. She's just upset it wasn't her idea," her mother assured me. "Come inside before the neighbors start snooping. Mrs. Claremont across the street is a nosy little bi--"

"Mother!" Maggie interjected. She rolled her eyes and walked back into the house. Her mother followed, defending herself and swinging her full skirt as she went.

I was left standing by the car with an overnight bag, wondering if Veronica had been right. A guy who looked about Maggie's age came and introduced himself. "June, Maggie's boyfriend. I hope you realize you're in for one hell of a weekend." He snickered. "Anything I can help you with?"

"There are Rice Krispie treats in the car, and a case of wine in the trunk."

"Nice! I'll grab the wine. Sweet ride," June said, whistling at my black Mercedes-Benz CL65.

"Yeah, thanks. Veronica wouldn't let me bring the convertible. She thought it was too flashy." It wasn't a complaint. The fact that Veronica was uncomfortable about my wealth just proved that she was indeed different from all the other women I'd dated.

She hadn't asked about my money at all, but sooner or later, it was a conversation we'd be having.

When I stepped inside the house, I felt surprisingly at peace. The living room had a floral couch, matching armchair, and a distressed coffee table. There were family photos and vintage pieces on a sideboard and lace curtains on the windows. Clearly Veronica had had a hand in decorating. There were stark differences between the home I'd grown up in and theirs.

However, the smell emanating from somewhere inside was slightly off, fighting against the sweet aroma of lit vanilla candles. I coughed as I got a good dose of the scent. Veronica shrieked. June and I looked at each other and followed the sound to the source.

Inside the bright kitchen, gray smoke wafted out of the open oven door, and the smell was more putrid than

27

it was from the living room. I dropped the bag on the floor, the tray of treats Veronica had made on the counter, and covered my mouth.

"I told you not to let her cook, Maggie."

Mrs. Stewart sat on a nearby chair, fanning herself with the hem of her long skirt, and exposing things I didn't need to see. I averted my eyes toward Maggie, who appeared ready to vomit as she yanked open a window.

"I tried, Nica! You know how she gets." Maggie covered her mouth, eyes tearing up.

"I'm right here, you know. How was I supposed to know that the plastic has to be removed? It just said put it on a tray, heat up the oven and stick it in," their mother reasoned.

When I was younger, I grew up away from my family when my brother and I attended boarding school. I'd never had to experience *this kind* of tension within a family. These days, there was barely any communication between my mother and me, if at all, and I preferred it that way. I pulled the collar of my cashmere sweater over my mouth to take a deep breath and grabbed a pair of oven mitts to help Veronica deal with the unidentifiable burnt blob.

Looking behind me, I saw June swipe at the tears flowing from his eyes. "Hey, can you get Maggie and Mrs. Stewart out of here? Open all the windows too." He nodded and led the two women out of the kitchen.

"This is why I didn't want her to cook." Veronica continued to fan the smoke out of the oven with a floral apron. I didn't know how she was able to stomach the fumes.

"Here, let me take care of that." I reached over and grabbed the ends of the tray. Trying as hard as I could not to take a deep breath, the acrid smell of burnt plastic attacked my senses. If I didn't get the blob out of here, I would soon lose my breakfast on the tiled kitchen floor. Although the taste of bile in my mouth would be an improvement.

"Where's the bin?" Veronica had a blank look on her face. "The garbage, love. Where's the garbage?"

"Oh! Through there." She pointed behind me at a white door.

I went through it and found what I was looking for. After dumping the blob in it and sealing the plastic by tying the end in a tight knot, I returned to the kitchen, leaving the door wide open. There wasn't anything we could do with the smell except let it air out.

With her forehead furrowed, she fumed, massaging her temples. "That was supposed to be dinner. Thank God we got here early. She could have burned the whole house down."

I remained silent, keeping a hand over half of my face.

"Now do you see why I was so nervous?" She propped a hand on her hip.

I sauntered over to her, ditching the mitts on the counter. Snaking my hand around her waist, I planted a kiss on her firmly pressed lips. "I'm sure we can remedy this. All I need is a grocery store."

"Tough luck. Nothing is open today."

"Nothing?"

"Haven't you been in America long enough to realize that?"

"Sorry, love, other people do the shopping for me."

Veronica pursed her lips. "Well, for us regular people, the stores close during National Holidays."

"Well then, I'll have to check what we have in hand."

"Yeah, good luck with that. Let's hope Maggie remembered to do the shopping yesterday."

"Oh, ye of little faith." I gave her another quick kiss. If I could fix this, it would earn me some major brownie points.

I grinned when I opened the fridge door. Brownie points galore!

KEEP CALM AND BE THANKFUL

VERONICA

*a*t this point, I was ready to get in Levi's car and drive back to San Francisco. If we were lucky, we could get there before night fell. Levi was adamant that he could save dinner, though. He was a fabulous cook, but I couldn't see how even he could perform a big enough miracle to pull it off.

I was also shocked he had packed properly. I'd been worried he might have thrown in just whatever for the weekend. I suspected he did it when I was in the shower (and he didn't join me). As I looked through the bag, I realized I should have known not to doubt him. Could he be any more perfect?

I had pajamas, matching undies, dresses, jeans, a sweater and a t-shirt, my face cream, toothbrush, and deodorant. I used whatever soap and shampoo were available, and Levi preferred me *au naturel*. No makeup needed.

His clothing was just as sparse. He did sleep in the

nude, but he'd brought two pairs of pajama bottoms for the weekend. In the bag were his personal items, clothes for the weekend, his glasses, and an old French book. There was nothing sexier than a man who reads.

I was getting all our stuff out when Mom walked into my bedroom with Maggie and June in tow. "You can't sleep in the same room."

I sent a "you can't be serious" look at Mom.

"Veronica, it's not setting a good example for your sister."

"I'm sure they're fine." I shot the couple a glance and found Maggie blushing. I shouldn't assume things. "And besides, Levi's working so damn hard downstairs making sure we'll have dinner after your attempt at cooking a turkey. I am not making him sleep on that lumpy couch."

"You can sleep on the couch then," my mother suggested.

I was about to say something when Maggie butted in. "Nica can sleep with me in my room. We'll have a sleepover just like old times, so Levi can have this bed."

My mother couldn't possibly think that was a horrible idea. She smiled brightly and took my and Maggie's hands and pulled us in a tight hug. "It's so good to have both of you girls in the house again."

After unpacking and ensuring the bed had clean sheets for Levi, I asked Maggie to set up the patio table with me. The smell from my mother's attempted dinner fought with the better-smelling food Levi was creating in the kitchen. It was going to be a bit chilly outdoors, so I brought blankets for everyone. I would brave the cold before choking on the gross smell that lurked in the whole house while we were eating.

I poked my head into the kitchen and found him bent over watching the oven door. *Mmm-hmmm.* It was hard not to stare at his sexy butt.

"Did you come in here to ogle me?" He stretched up slowly and glanced over his shoulder.

I sauntered over to him. "I came here to do this." I gave his butt a squeeze. "And this." And placed a kiss on his lips. Levi responded by holding me close to him, wrapping his strong arms around me, pressing his hips forward, and taking my breath away.

There was nothing sexier than a man who read and cooked and kissed like it was our last day on earth.

His hands roved over my hips when we heard the kitchen door slam.

"Oh my gawd!" a squeaky voice interrupted us.

Delaney was one of my sister's friends. She was nothing like Maggie. She had her nails constantly painted, packed makeup on her face, showed a little too much skin, and last I'd heard, had dated half the guys in the football team—everything Maggie wasn't. Delaney eyed Levi up and down like she was ready to lick him clean.

"What are you doing here, Delaney?" I refused to let go of Levi.

Delaney slowly trailed her eyes to me, like she'd just found out I existed. "Maggie said your mom cooked, so my mom told be to bring you this. Brussels sprouts. Yech!" She lifted a bowl covered with plastic wrap.

Levi stretched out a hand and took it from her.

"These are perfect." He lifted the cover and sniffed the bowl. "With bacon. Brussels sprouts are my favorite."

"Really?" Delaney's voice went up a bit higher. "Mine too!" She even batted her lashes.

"Thanks, Delaney, Maggie and June are out back." I stared at her until she got the point, and finally, she traipsed out of the kitchen after sending Levi a flirty wink.

"Neighbor?" Levi asked, turning to do a quick check on whatever was in the oven.

"No, Maggie's best friend."

"Really?"

"See, you don't even know her, and you find that odd. Maggie's very friendly and she's popular at school. But there's something about Delaney that I can't quite figure out." I tapped my finger on my lips. Levi pushed it away and kissed me.

"Dinner will be ready in ten minutes. It's not turkey, but I promise you it's good."

"Sounds great. After that smell, I don't know if I will ever have turkey ever again." I gave him another kiss (and squeeze) before heading back to the patio.

RECONNAISSANT

LEVI

The last dinner I had with my family in France was when I'd turned eight. There had been plenty of food then, but it wasn't as nearly enjoyable as this—a real family dinner full of warmth, laughter and shared memories.

I'd tried my best with what I was given: eggs, milk, an uncanny amount of processed cheese, bread and vegetables. The meal wasn't gourmet, but thankfully, they all seemed to like it. And nobody choked.

With the blankets and cushions Veronica brought out to the patio, everyone was comfortable. Flowers in old teacups and colored glasses dotted the middle of the table, surrounding a medium-sized pumpkin, and weaved around it were candles in different sizes. Despite the chill, it was a cloudless night and the stars added to the ambiance.

I'd never celebrated Thanksgiving. Year after year, I'd ignored it like any other holiday meant for spending time with family, and had spent time with whichever woman wanted to be with me instead.

Veronica and Maggie cleaned up while their mother changed into something less formal. June and I sat in the living room and watched his football games on video. He didn't talk much, and when he did, it was only about football, but he was pleasant company.

To my dismay, as we retreated to our bedrooms, I found out I wouldn't be sleeping in the same bed as Veronica. But we were at her mother's house, and her mother had strict rules. If I were to prove I belonged with Veronica, I'd have to follow those rules.

However, while stretching on what used to be Veronica's bed, I craved her warmth and the steady beating of her heart. And her soft kisses, her touch. The taste of her. The sweet scent I would never tire of.

Turning on my side, I punched the pillow in frustration and huffed a heavy breath. I had to stop thinking of her and what she could do to me or I'd be faced with more than lack of sleep. Then I heard the creaking of the hardwood floors outside the pink and purple bedroom. I propped myself up, reached over to turn on the lamp, and pulled the sheets to cover my bottom half before the door opened.

"Hi." Veronica gingerly snuck into the room and closed the door behind her. She crawled into bed in that sexy way that drove me wild, with her butt in the air and a wicked smile playing at her lips.

"What are you doing here? I thought you weren't allowed..." She didn't let me finish. She swooped in and kissed me like it was our last time on earth.

"I can't sleep without you," she said after letting us breathe.

"Me too."

After turning off the lamp, Veronica curled in beside me, reached for my arm, wrapped it around her, and intertwined our fingers. I nuzzled her neck before burrowing my nose in her hair. Our feet tangled under the sheets. I was warmed. Comforted. Loved.

Her breathing became steady. I inhaled her sweet scent as my eyes started to droop close.

"Thanks for saving Thanksgiving," she said in her sleepy, hushed voice.

"You're welcome," I said and smiled against her hair.

I never understood why Americans felt they had to stuff themselves silly every year like they did on Thanksgiving. But tonight, having eaten dinner with Veronica and her family, I realized that it was about more than the food. It was about togetherness. It was about family and those they loved, a concept that was alien to me.

Although Veronica thought I had saved Thanksgiving, what she didn't know was that she had saved me. And I would forever be grateful to her for that.

BAGUE DE FIANÇAILLES

LEVI

A few months later...

"Will she say yes?"

Martina regarded me with her scrupulous gray eyes when she asked the question. Her silver hair was effortlessly pulled back into a chignon. Wrinkles lined where they should on a seventy-two-year-old woman's face. There wasn't a hint of that ever-present playful smile, not that our conversation was anything to laugh at.

"You don't trust that I know the answer?" I said in a steady voice, leaning my tensed back against the chair.

Martina lifted the small, square box and studied it, as though it hadn't been in her possession for decades.

"I'm surprised, that of all people, it was you who'd asked for this. No one else dared." This was common knowledge in my family: only Martina had worn it for years. My mother wouldn't have considered wearing it despite what it represented; the ring was too simple for her taste.

Martina raised a thin eyebrow at me. "I didn't think you had it in you."

I'd been the first one to turn away from any semblance of commitment in the past. Martina had witnessed it year after year, relationship after relationship. The closest I'd gotten to a real relationship was with my ex, Natalie, but even she knew whatever we had wouldn't last, and we'd decided we were better as friends than lovers.

"Will you at least let me meet her?" There was a hint of hope in her voice, though she would never admit to it.

I scoffed, rubbing the three-day growth on my jaw. "I don't know if I can trust you with her. What if you turn her against me?"

"If I could do that, then she isn't the right woman for you," she challenged me, with an eyebrow raised and her chin lifted. Her words struck a chord. However, my trepidation wasn't if Veronica was the right woman for me, but if I was right for her. If I was good enough, worthy enough.

Taking my eyes away from my grandmother, I watched the men and women working in the vineyards through the terrace doors. The sun peeked behind cumulus clouds, and the heat wasn't bothersome: a perfect day for a green harvest. Martina predicted that it would be a successful year for the entire region. She was rarely wrong when it came to these matters. Only a handful of people had her skills. She loved to pretend that it was all guesswork, but I had seen her work. It wasn't an exact science, but with a bit of luck and years of experience, she had created a working formula.

She'd also been right about a lot of my past romantic interludes. Though I knew she would never interfere with my current relationship, she would scrutinize it to pieces. I couldn't let her do that this time. Not that I was afraid she would find something amiss with Veronica.

There's no such thing as a perfect relationship, but what I had with Veronica was damn near perfect. She came into my life like a breath of fresh air, when I was already suffocating. When I finally admitted that there was something missing in my life. I hoped that it could only get better from here. That I could lay my own insecurities to rest.

"Make sure you get it back if it doesn't work out. We can't forget what happened to Alexandre. Imagine if he'd given her this." Martina replaced the box on the painted table, and slid it my way. I caught it before it dropped to the floor.

A dry laugh escaped me. "You just had to, didn't you?" Any mention of my brother was a sore subject. I opened the box, took the ring out and examined it in the light. "After everything that happened, did we expect her family to give back anything Alexandre had given her?" My chest tightened.

It had been in my family for years, and since there was no sign of Alex ever returning to our lives—not that

I wanted him to—it only felt right that I asked for it. No matter how much doubt came from Martina. It would mean a lot to me if…when Veronica decided to wear it, having it represent our commitment to each other. And it could bring us luck, just as it had to my grandparents —the only couple I knew who'd stayed with each other until death.

She stood and walked over to me. Her left foot dragged slightly on the floor, and it took her longer to get anywhere with the pain she experienced, the pain she would never talk about, pain that I couldn't easily ignore. She cradled my head between her hands, and made me tilt my face up, much like she had done when I was a little boy. "Remember, Olivier: *l'amour fait les plus grandes douceurs et les plus sensibles infortunes de la vie.*"

I chuckled and patted her hands. "Love brings both the greatest delicacies and the most sensitive misfortunes in life. Wise old saying, Onna. Is that from experience?"

She tutted and shook a dainty finger at me. "I told you not to call me that! Onna…you make me sound so old." Then she kissed the top of my head. "I worry about you."

"You shouldn't. There is a fine, young woman who's taking great care of me these days." I patted her hands again, and held them in my own, making her look me straight in the eye so that she could understand the seriousness of what I was about to say. "I'm not coming back to live here again and take over. I'm doing well on my own. You should quit hoping."

"We'll see, Olivier, we shall see." Martina never liked not getting her way.

I worried about her and how the pitfalls of her age had started to show more and more these past years. She'd been expressing her desire to have me back in Bordeaux a lot lately, and I'd agonized over it. If all I would come back to were this vineyard and Martina, I'd have done it years ago. But my family had as much drama as an American soap opera, and more complications as well. I realized that one day soon, Veronica would ask more about my family here in France.

I'd only shared the fundamentals, those that couldn't hurt us.

Veronica might be a levelheaded, patient, and understanding woman, but my family was beyond reproachful. My intentions were, and had always been, to be with her as long as I possibly could. Exposing her to my family would be detrimental to that plan.

No, no way in hell would she ever come here and meet them, not even Martina, the only trustworthy person in my family.

&.

VERONICA HAD LEFT a lamp on in the living room, illuminating a good portion of her apartment when I came in. I wished she would listen and let me get her a dog, something vicious-looking that could rip through flesh. Or she could move in with me sooner rather than later.

Tired from my travels, I groaned. I slipped the box out of my jacket pocket and lifted the lid. The three-point-five karat, off-white rock glimmered even in the sparse light. I would have to have it cleaned before presenting it to her so she could appreciate the filigree designs on the band. It was beautiful. It was delicate. It was one of a kind, much like Veronica, *amour de ma vie*. Love of my life. And once she said 'yes', I could have our initials engraved inside the band, right beside Martina's and Philippe's.

I didn't take a lot of stock on family traditions. Veronica would more than appreciate the simple yet elegant designs of the ring. But since it came from Martina, it meant more to me. It was my family's ring. *My* ring on Veronica. Her wearing it would solidify our relationship. It would mean she'd be mine for as long as she'd have me. And I intended to have her in my life forever.

I returned the ring to the box and left it in my coat pocket. Veronica wasn't the type to go snooping around. It would be safe in there, and the surprise would be kept.

I had a lot of planning to do. How could one propose to the most romantic, most thoughtful and loving woman in the world? If I had been another person, I would have hired her to come up with a plan with me. I laughed at myself. That would be something to tell our children: "I tricked your mother to helping me plan my proposal for her." It would require a lot of thought every step of the way. It needed to be perfect, a gesture so grand she couldn't say no.

I padded to the bedroom. After undressing, I crawled into bed and felt her stir, aware of my presence. It was a connection we shared. Circling my arms around her, I brought her closer to me, and she moved into the curve I'd created with my body, where she fit perfectly. Where she belonged.

Burying my nose in her curls, her scent ignited my nerves. Her chest rose and fell, and her heart beat steadily, such a contrast to the faster beating of mine. I should let her sleep.

Veronica muttered my name. I missed her. Every minute I'd been away from her had been spent thinking about her. Of her body against mine. Of the different sensations that only she could make me feel. The passion. The fire. The undeniable love.

Her fingers tangled with mine, and our joined hands pressed against her chest. She lifted one leg and wrapped it around mine underneath the sheets, bringing me even closer to her. I was feverish, keenly aflame. I breathed her in once more, kissing the delicate skin behind her ear, and felt the electricity surge, flowing from me to her and her to me.

"Welcome back home," she whispered in the dark.

Home. The word had taken a different meaning, a different form ever since she had told me she loved me. Home had always been nothing but a physical location for me in the past. With her, home was where I left my heart. And my heart belonged to her.

Without her, I was lost.

In that moment, as I kissed the pulse on her neck, her hands bringing me closer, I knew without a doubt that I had made the right decision of asking Martina for the ring. All I had to do was come up with the perfect proposal and when Veronica agreed, I would forevermore be the luckiest man on earth. I would forevermore be home. And I would forevermore be loved.

LE TÉMOIN DU MARIÉ

*H*alf-dazed, I searched for Veronica, reaching a hand over her part of the bed. When my hands touched cold sheets, my eyes popped open. I turned on my back and looked around the room.

The sun filtered through the windows and a soft wind ruffled the floral curtains. On one side of the room, the en suite bathroom door was wide open, meaning Veronica had finished showering and dressing for work. Had I missed her? She could be as quiet as a thief in the night when getting ready in the mornings. Pushing the quilt off me, I swung my legs over the bed and padded out of the bedroom, rubbing a hand over my face.

She was still in the apartment, in the kitchen, already dressed for work. I paused at the threshold as Veronica swore at the espresso machine I'd brought over the week before. The fact that she was making coffee instead of tea meant she was exhausted, too. I almost regretted that I had woken her up when I came home. Almost.

I approached her from behind, letting my hands wander over her curves, and tasting the fragrance of the exposed skin of her neck and shoulder. "Good morning."

Her soft hum rumbled against my chest. She reached a hand up to tangle her fingers through my hair. "Did I wake you? I was trying to be quiet." She turned around, sucking in a gasp at my lack of clothes and my state of...readiness. Slowly dragging her eyes up to my face, she chewed on her bottom lip, and muttered, "I have to be at work in half an hour."

How could I resist? "I'll try very hard to get you to work on time."

"That's what you said last week, and I came in two hours late."

"I said I'll try," I murmured before hoisting her up, wrapping her legs around my hips, and supporting her bottom. With a Cheshire–cat grin on my face, I carried her back to bed.

THREE HOURS LATER, I watched as a black ball bounced on the wall an inch below the outline and flew my way. I waited for the right moment to swing my racket, making contact with the ball right after it hit the floor once.

As highly competitive individuals, Jake and I could get into serious relays. However, not once had he beat

ot in squash. I wiped sweat off my
forehead, readying for another swing. And missed.

Admittedly, I was out of sorts. I was distracted.

I grunted, hitting the ball back toward the front wall.
It changed trajectory and shot past Jake's racket, less
than an inch away. But a miss was a miss. And it had
won me the game.

"You got lucky," Jake commented, as we walked to
the locker room.

"If you mean last night, yeah." I offered him a smirk.
"This morning too, if you must know. I might even drop
in on her after lunch at work."

Jake shook his head, grinning. "I meant that last
shot. My hand slipped." He was always a sore loser.
"Although I'm glad to know the honeymoon phase
hasn't ended."

"Far from it." I was proud to say it. Every single day
I'd spent with Veronica had been better than the one
before, but something niggled at me. Something I could
only describe as doubt and fear.

I opened my locker door and used a towel to swipe
off sweat before taking off my clothes. At first, I didn't
notice Jake staring at me. I paused, securing a large
towel over my hips.

"What?" I challenged.

"I never thought I'd see the day," Jake declared,
"Olivier Laurent, head over heels in love."

We had a unique situation, Jake and I. He'd dated
Veronica for a few months. They'd been exclusive, but
Veronica had been more serious about it than Jake. If he
were any other guy, and not my best friend, I would

8

have swung a left hook for hurting her when they broke up. I also could have been faulted for that since Jake had met Sandrine through me. In my defense, I'd not foreseen Jake falling for Sandrine the second they'd met.

At any other time, if Jake had admitted to falling in love that fast, I would have laughed at him and told him he'd lost his marbles. But eight months before Jake met Veronica, nearly a year before he and Sandrine had been introduced, I'd discovered that love at first sight existed.

Or, in my case, love at first bump. And every time I thought of that initial contact with Veronica, my blood pressure would spike.

But fate was cruel to me, always had been, despite the fact that everyone else thought otherwise. I had trouble—for the first time in my life—trying to connect with Veronica, or at the very least, have her notice me. I'd gone to event after event that she and her company had put together, almost feeling like a stalker.

Then one night, at yet another event, after a quick handshake with me, Jake had made a beeline for her, and they'd instantly hit it off. It had been painful observing them from afar. I'd tried drowning my sorrows with other women, acting like a complete buffoon around Jake and Veronica as they continued with their relationship.

All of that came to a stop when he broke it off and began dating my cousin, Sandrine. Veronica had even planned their wedding. During the planning, fate had finally smiled upon me.

Veronica had fought it, naturally.

"Are you going to give me an answer today?" Jake's question pierced through my thoughts.

"Did you ask me something?"

Jake laughed. "I asked if you're joining us at my parents on Thursday night."

"Ah, yeah, Thursday, sure." I scratched the top of my head. "For what again?"

"What the hell has gotten into you?" Jake laughed again. "I know you're probably not getting enough rest, but have mercy on Nica. She needs a good dose of sleep."

"What? I let her sleep...afterwards," I protested.

"Then what the hell has gotten into you?" There was an entertained look on his face, but a second later, it changed into something more serious. "Jesus, Levi, don't tell me you're thinking of breaking up with her!" He punched my right arm, though not hard. "You just told me that it was far from over?"

"No! Shit no! It's nothing like that."

"Then what is it?" Jake leaned forward, and lowered his voice. "Is she pregnant?"

"No! I don't think so." I couldn't exactly count how many times Veronica and I had made love, but every single time we'd been careful. "That's not it."

Jake spread his hands in front of him, waiting for an explanation.

I brushed my hair back, and reached into my locker. Jake looked down at the box I'd opened. "You're getting married?"

He made a movement that told me he was ready to give me a congratulations bump, but I stopped him. "I haven't asked her yet, genius." I snapped the box closed and returned it in my jacket pocket.

"She's going to say yes. You can't think that she won't."

I scratched the stubble on my face. I should shave. Veronica liked it when I shaved, but I also liked the little giggles she would release when a bit of facial hair tickled her.

"That's not what I'm worried about," I confessed, but it felt like a lie.

"What are you waiting for?"

My hands flew in the air. "It's the how." Jake didn't seem to understand. As much as he was charming, he wasn't the most romantic man. I'd had to help him plan his proposal to Sandrine. "It has to be perfect."

Jake clapped a hand on my shoulder. "I'm surprised you had it in you, considering everything." I tried not to think of what he meant by 'everything'.

"Ask Sandrine for ideas, or go to Chase. She'd be able to lead you to the right direction."

"Chase hates my guts."

Jake shrugged. "That's Chase, though. When it comes to Nica, she's like an overprotective watchdog, ready to pounce and draw blood."

My phone vibrated in my locker. A text message from Martina, asking if I had popped the question yet. (Reading between the lines: have I failed yet?) I shoved the phone back into the locker, slammed the door, and proceeded to the showers.

I WALKED through the Bliss Event Designers doors and was immediately greeted by Jewel, Veronica's colleague.

"She's in a meeting," she informed me, waving a hand toward the little square room they dubbed a "conference room".

"That's fine. Can I wait in her office?"

"Uhm...she has another client waiting there." Jewel leaned her hands on her small desk. "He's been waiting for half an hour. I tried to reschedule him, but he was insistent."

I glanced at Veronica's office. The blinds on the windows were not drawn, shielding whoever was inside from me, and the door was closed. I wasn't thrilled to find out that she'd be alone in her office with another man. Not that I didn't trust her. I did, implicitly. It was always the other person I couldn't trust. With a past like mine, it was hard to avoid trust issues.

"I'll sit out here then. You don't mind if I make a few phone calls, do you?" Jewel shook her head. "Thanks, I promise to do it quietly."

I took a spot on the comfortable gray couch beside the large window, dropping the paper bag and bouquet of flowers I carried on the glass coffee table in front of me. Before I could go through my contacts, a text message from Veronica appeared on the screen:

Hey, hot stuff!

Grinning at the phone, I sent a quick reply:

Hey yourself, gorgeous. I miss you.

Peering through my lashes, I spied her looking casual, pretty in her pink floral dress, and unaffected by my text, while she listened to what her client was saying.

I love that dress on you. What happened to the blue dress from this morning?

I watched her surreptitiously read my text, reddening at my implication, and typing on her phone under the table:

Someone wrinkled it. Then he made me late for work AGAIN!

Rubbing my chin with a hand, I hid my smirk behind my fingers, before I typed back:

Lucky bastard.

I waited for another reply but when I looked up, she'd taken over the meeting. Instead of making phone calls, I replied to emails that had been waiting for me.

Five minutes later, Chase, Veronica, and their clients stepped out of the conference room. Veronica bade them farewell and walked them to the door before standing before me. She bent down and placed a quick kiss on my lips. Her lips tasted like honey.

"I brought you lunch." I pointed at the table.

Veronica looked over her shoulder, turned around and picked up the flowers, pressing the peonies to her nose. "And flowers! How romantic. Your mother taught you well." I smiled at her. It was a simple gesture that I didn't learn from my mother, nor from my father. My mother had constantly stated that there wasn't a romantic bone in my father…at least not toward her. He had shown all of that to women he'd cheated with.

"Thank you for lunch, but I have another meeting,"

she said, pointing at her closed office door. "Can you wait in the kitchen? I'll try to keep it short."

I stood, nodding. "I'm in no rush. The food will keep."

"Great," Veronica said as she sauntered to her office. The sway of her hips mesmerized me. I could never get enough of watching her.

{♣.}

I WAS SEATED on one of the four stools in the kitchen, reading the local paper, when Chase walked in.

The ring was in my pocket, and I patted it for reassurance. Checking to see that Veronica hadn't emerged from her office, I cleared my throat and talked to her best friend. "Chase, I was wondering if you have a moment to spare?"

She didn't pause or make a sound while she stirred sugar into her coffee.

I tried again. "It doesn't have to be today. But sometime soon." That, somehow, went through to her.

"Whatever cockamamie plan you have, I don't want any part of it." I opened my mouth to protest but she continued, "Her birthday is not for another three months. And there aren't any major holidays coming up. So whatever it is, keep me out of it."

"Please, it's important."

Chase took a deep breath in, and looked up to the ceiling as though she had run out of patience. She turned to face me, cleared the two steps to the bar-height table I was seated at, and pointed an accusatory finger at me. "I should have said this before but I didn't because I kept a promise to Nica. But enough is enough." She narrowed her eyes at me and leaned even closer. "I don't like you. I don't trust you. You are Jake's best friend, and look what he did to Nica. I am *not* going to let you destroy the best person I know. If you hurt her--"

"I'm going to ask her to marry me."

She stepped back, as though I'd pushed her with my words. She twisted her lips, and confusion colored her face. "You what?"

Veronica's unmistakable, infectious laugh came from the front of the office. Her office door was ajar but she hadn't stepped out yet.

As fast as I could, I told Chase, "I can't talk about it now, but I *will* need your help, please. "

Chase narrowed her eyes at me again, studying me with speculation. "Fine. I'll send you a text tomorrow."

"Thank you." I would have hugged her, but she might have bitten my head off. Instead, I stretched a hand out. Chase only stared at my proffered hand, and scoffed at me before walking out of the kitchen after grabbing her coffee.

I followed her out and watched Veronica walk a man out of her office. She had to tilt her chin up while talking to him. He looked vaguely familiar but I couldn't place him. Veronica had a bright smile on her face, and so did he. My hands fisted at my sides when he leaned down to place a kiss on her cheek, lingering too long for my liking, and worse, causing her cheeks to redden.

What the hell? Who was this man who could make

her blush? Every bit of me wanted to plow through the small office and pummel the man to the ground. I resisted, of course.

I looked away when Chase snickered behind me.

I ignored her as Veronica approached. "Sorry. It took longer than necessary."

"Not a big deal," I managed to say through gritted teeth.

We walked into the kitchen, where I had her lunch waiting. Sitting in front of her at the table, I bit the inside of my cheek. A part of me was saying I should let it go, and the other part niggled at me to ask. The latter won. "New client?"

Veronica hummed, digging into her salad with her fork.

"Who is he? I've seen him before." My voice was steady. Firm.

Too firm. If Veronica didn't think I was jealous before, she did now.

As she poked a piece of tomato with her fork, she replied with, "Can't talk about it. Did you bring me some bread?"

And with that, the topic was closed for discussion. I waited for her to glance up at me, to give some kind of explanation, but she didn't offer any. When she did look up, she seemed nervous. I patted my pocket again.

TÉMOIN DE MARIAGE

"First off, I don't like to keep secrets from Nica." Chase's steady finger met me before I stepped out of my car. "I'm only doing this because she loves surprises. And she happens to love you. I don't know why." She looked me up and down with a sneer. "But she does. If you mess this up..."

"Could you at least retract your claws until after we talk about what we came here for?"

"I'm warning you, Laurent. I will castrate you,'" Chase carefully enunciated the last two words.

"I'm very much aware." If I grinned even a smidgen, she might take a tire iron to my kneecaps. "Shall we?" I waved a hand toward the bar by the pier.

The pungent mixture of briny sea air and stale beer hung in the air as we walked inside the dodgy bar, Davidson's. It was easy to figure out why Chase had asked to meet here. She wanted the upper hand. It was a bikers' hang out. With her black leather clothes with metal rivets and studs, and her even darker demeanor, she looked like she belonged. While I, in my checkered Oxfords, navy suit, and caramel brogues, was conspicuous.

I followed her to the banged-up, scratched wood-and-steel bar. She occupied one of the empty stools in front of a hulk of a man with a salt-and-pepper beard that matched the mop on top of his head.

Chase postured beside me, placing her helmet on top of the bar. "Three Floyds stout."

The giant, bearded man grunted at my grinning companion, and focused on me. I couldn't ignore Chase's outright enjoyment of what she certainly suspected was my discomfort as I sat next to her. I pushed my hair off my forehead and extended my hand.

"*Bonjour, Benoit. Comment ca va?*" I greeted the burly man. I repeated my last question in English, "How are things?"

He returned my greeting with a more convivial one, taking my hand in a complicated handshake. "*Olivier, pas mal! Quoi de neuf?*"

It was regular exchange between two people. I wasn't saying anything that would matter to Chase, but it irritated her, and I couldn't help but egg her on. "*Pas grand-chose. Nous parlerons plus tard.*" She was practically vibrating in her seat in anger. "Macallan, neat."

Benoit saluted me and knocked once on the bench before turning around and grabbing our drinks. Chase huffed as she grabbed her tall glass of foamy beer and her helmet and stalked away from the bar toward the farthest empty booth. I swallowed a chuckle. Benoit would have a ton of questions for me later. How could I explain Chase? I didn't even know her last name. I'd asked Veronica a while ago about it, and she had shrugged. "Think Madonna. And Cher," was her explanation.

"You're a jerk. Why didn't you tell me you know this place?" If Chase knew how to pout, she would have. She glared at me, a furrow in her forehead, most likely imagining ways of kicking my ass.

I was the bar's silent investor. Bikers like spending money on beer, and they made loyal clientele. With the margins the place made, it had proven to be a great investment.

I slid in the booth across from her, taking a sip of my scotch before shrugging. "You'd be surprised who I know in this city."

Chase scoffed. "We're never gonna get anywhere. Tell me what you're planning to do." Before I could answer, she continued, "Nica loves surprises. The bigger, the better. Don't cheap out on anything, because she deserves only the best. She's probably the best person in this entire state. She's my best friend, my family. If it wasn't for her, I honestly don't know where I would be. I want her to be happy." She paused as though she was entertaining a thought, or she felt she had exposed herself a bit much to me, of all people. "Her ring size is five, and you have to get her mother's blessing, whether you believe in that or not."

I had had the idea in my head, but I hadn't been too sure. Perhaps this was why I'd bitten back my pride and asked to meet with Chase. "I'm on my way to see Lily

MICHELLE JO QUINN

after this. I'm driving out to meet her at work." And the other reason why I'd insisted that I meet Chase earlier in the day. It had taken her a while to agree with me, but she had relented.

"Oh. Well, that's good." I didn't think it was possible, but for once, she was speechless, and I could almost believe that she might even be impressed.

"Is there anything else you could tell me that you think only you would know?"

This was a long shot. She could tell me what I needed to know or deliberately mislead me. In a way, I could even perceive that I was sabotaging myself. Would I be asking this question if I truly knew who Veronica was? And wasn't that one of the prerequisites of asking a woman to marry me?

But Veronica wasn't just any woman. She was the *one* for me. I believed it.

I needed to make this proposal perfect.

Chase lifted her glass and drank half of the beer. She regarded me with her arms folded over her chest. I leaned against the padded booth, waiting for her answer.

"Nope. Nothing that I want to share."

I shook my head. What else could I have expected? Chase finished off the beer in one pull and slammed the empty glass on the table. I signaled Benoit to bring her another. I had a feeling it would take a lot more than one to make her talk.

"Tell me, Laurent, what's your plan?"

"My plan?" She lifted a brow and pursed her lips. "Right, my plan." I leaned my arms over the table, bravely facing my surly companion with a deep breath before I began sharing.

§&

THE COOL AIR hit my face as I slid out of the top-down convertible. The fog had been fairly thick throughout the drive and it had taken a lot longer for me to arrive at my destination. When I walked into the store, I didn't expect a slew of shoppers, considering it was just past noon.

"Levi?" Mrs. Stewart's surprised voice piped up from my left. She looked at me over her glasses. "It is you! What are you doing here?"

She was a hugger. And so I bent down to let her wrap her arms around me and pat my face.

"Hello, Mrs. Stewart." I straightened as soon as I was sure she had patted my cheeks enough.

"How many times do I have to tell you to call me Lily? Mrs. Stewart makes me sound old." She shook a finger at me, and smiled. I wondered briefly how she'd get on with my mother. Not that it would ever happen. Mother was offensive even at her best behavior, but Lily wasn't a person anyone should mess with. Having raised two daughters on her own, she'd admitted that she'd had to be stronger than most.

"Of course. I beg your pardon. How are you, Lily?"

"I'm good. Just getting this place together."

"I was hoping I could steal you for a minute to discuss something?" Lily squinted. "It's nothing bad. It'll be quick, I hope."

"Alright, dear. Follow me, we'll have a chat in my office." I walked beside her to a door marked "OF ICE", while she greeted customers and employees, each one smiling at her and giving me a curious once-over.

She offered a chair that looked like it was there even before the store was, and she pulled a similar, less beat-up one to sit on. "Is it about my daughter? Is she acting up?"

"Not at all. Veronica and I are doing well."

"Well, go on, tell me." Lily waved her hand, rolling her wrist to encourage me to continue.

Why did I suddenly feel nervous? I pulled my handkerchief from an inside coat pocket and rubbed my palms on it. I took a couple of soothing breaths before talking.

"I'd like to ask for your daughter's hand in marriage. I'd like your blessing." My eyes trained on Lily.

She didn't answer. I thought I'd repeat myself, in case she hadn't heard me, but as I opened my mouth, she lifted a finger.

"I don't understand," she told me.

"I intend to ask your daughter, Veronica, to marry me. Soon, I hope."

"But why are you asking for my permission?"

Now I was confused. "I thought it was the right thing to do?" I hadn't meant it to come out as a question.

"It might be for other girls, but not my Nica."

"How do you mean?"

Lily took off her glasses and pinched the bridge of her nose. Waiting for her reply, I watched her clean the lenses with the bottom of her cotton shirt before she put them back on. "Levi, my Nica is a modern woman. If she finds out that you'd come here to ask for her hand in marriage, she might go and break it off."

"But…"

"Oh, please tell me Chase did not put you up to this! Just make sure Nica doesn't find out." She reached over to pat my hand. "Veronica believes that no man would ever own her. She is her own person. She may seem weak or timid at times, but she is neither. She's a strong, independent woman." She pressed her lips together. I kept quiet. There was more to come. "When she was little, girls her age played with Barbies. My Nica read books and feminist magazines that my neighbor across the street shared with her."

"I didn't realize."

"I know. I used to joke that she was two people in one little body. But you go ask her to marry you. I bet she would say yes. She would be stupid not to. But make sure that she doesn't get wind of this." She whirled a finger in the air.

Lily stood slowly, and I did the same. How had I been wrong? I had been sure Veronica would have wanted this. Lily and I shuffled outside the office, and she practically threw me out of the store, saying that she had work to do. *How could I have gotten this wrong?* I wondered again. How could Chase have? Or could it be that her mother was wrong about Veronica? They seemed at odds with each other at times.

I was halfway back to San Francisco when I realized that Lily hadn't even hugged me before I left. It was unusual. I reached for the panel on the dash and searched through my contacts for Chase's number, but as I was about to connect, Veronica's number popped up. I pressed the button to answer.

"Sweetheart, hi."

Her voice exploded in my car. "Babe! Oh my god, I'm so excited. I'm working on something big, and I think I'm going to get it."

Her excitement was infectious, and I found myself grinning. "Glad to hear it. What are you working on?"

Her voice turned into a more delicate tone. "I can't tell you that, but it's huge. And there's something else I have to tell you."

"Go on."

"I have to do some traveling in the next two weeks. All expenses paid."

"Two weeks?"

"Yes, and I...kinda have to leave the day after tomorrow."

"In two days?" I gripped my steering wheel harder. "But we're going to the Benjamin's' for dinner on Thursday." Even to me, I sounded whiney.

Veronica sighed heavily through the speakerphone. "Yeah. I can't go to that anymore. I already told Sandrine. I told them you'd still be there."

"Two weeks. You'll be gone that long? I'm going to miss you. Can we talk about this later? Dinner at my place?"

"Yeah, sounds good. I'll see you later. I have some prep to do since I'll be gone quite a while."

"I understand. I'll make something great tonight. Who are you going with?"

Even without seeing her, I sensed her hesitation. "A client." A pregnant pause. "He's taking me to see some spots for an event."

"He?"

"Yes?"

I couldn't resist. I didn't know what pushed me. "The same person you had a meeting with yesterday afternoon?"

Her silence was my answer. My knuckles whitened as I squeezed the steering wheel. "I can't say much about it, but yes." Her voice had lowered even more.

"Is Chase going?"

"No. Chase doesn't fly anywhere. And he's my client." Her voice turned edgier, more defensive. "My project. Look, we can talk more later. I have to go. I love you."

I exhaled. I knew she would hear nothing but tension in my voice. "I love you too."

I didn't like the idea of Veronica spending weeks alone with this man.

🐚

"I'LL BE BACK before you know it," I heard Veronica say, but all I could focus on was the amount of clothes she had piled into her suitcase. I'd counted at least seven bathing suits, and five were two-piece affairs. I watched her fold several pairs of lace underwear and stuff them along the side.

"What do you need those for?" I rubbed the back of my neck, trying to ease the tension.

Veronica peered at me through her lashes, a confused smile on her face. "My panties?" She threw back her head and laughed. "Would you prefer I go commando the entire two weeks?"

No, I preferred she not go at all. But there was no stopping her.

She rounded the bed and stepped between my legs. Her nose touched mine as she cupped my chin with her hands. "Why are you so worked up over this? It's just work."

"Why can't you tell me who he is?"

"Levi, I've told you why. It's part of the deal. He asked for confidentiality. And I can't believe you're still trying to ask. You have nothing to worry about." Her soothing voice reverberated down my chest as she covered my lips with hers. Her tongue danced with mine, and I inhaled every bit of her. I let my hands rub and rove up her naked legs, under the hem of her blue dress. My fingers skimmed the silk and lace covering the roundness of her behind.

"I have to go." She said the words, but her fingers pushed through my hair and tugged as my lips found the hollow of her neck.

She could have been trying to distract me, but I was willing to make the sacrifice. Too many things had come between us in the past that could've prevented us from being together, including our stubborn selves.

"Babe, Jewel is coming to get me soon." I had

already removed the barrier between me and what I wanted, slipping silk and lace material down her legs.

"I won't take long," I promised, laying her on the floral quilt beside the opened suitcase. Her dress was halfway up her hips. "You'll be gone a while, I want to make sure you'll think of me...and only me...."

I hurried to remove my clothes, depositing them on the floor, and helped her take her dress off. The only thing left to do was to unsnap the lace bra that matched the panties I had disposed of earlier.

"Hurry." Veronica reached for me, and I let her guide me where she desired me most.

That was when the knock came. I looked past the open bedroom door and gave an angry huff into Veronica's hair.

"That's Jewel. I told you she'd be here soon." She made no move to push me off.

"I'll fly you to the Maldives myself." I buried my face in the curve of her neck, inhaling her scent.

Another knock echoed into the apartment, followed by the buzzing of her phone on the nightstand. There wasn't any fear of anyone walking in on us. Since an embarrassing, yet unforgettable, incident with her mother and sister on Christmas, Veronica had asked people to call her first before zipping into her apartment.

"Levi, babe, look at me." Veronica ran her fingers on my neck, urging me to lift my head up and stare her in the eyes. She trapped my head between her hands. "I love you." The spark in her eyes reaffirmed her words. "I will miss you, but it's only two weeks. I will call you, Skype, FaceTime, whatever you want, every single free time I get. Jewel will be with me. I won't be alone with my client the entire time. Then, I will come back home to you, where I belong."

She rubbed a thumb over one of my cheeks and down my chin. Her thumb traced the outline of my lips, as though she was committing it to memory. I captured her thumb between my teeth and when I gently sucked, she moaned. It was like I was struck by lightning.

I'd been with different women for many reasons, treating each relationship like a business. I had only known real love with Veronica.

My heart swelled at her words, at her promises. She lifted her head to plant another heat-searing kiss on my lips. I met it with all the fervor and passion I could manage. Then, slowly, I turned to my side, freeing her, and helped her up to let her redress.

She was mine, and I was hers.

I stayed quiet the entire time, kicking myself for not bringing the ring. Although the time wasn't perfect, I would've wanted her wearing the ring before she went to an island with another man...to let him know that she was with me.

The limo her client had provided idled outside the apartment as I held her one more time.

"C'mon, lovebirds, we're going to miss that first flight," Jewel informed us as we stood by the door.

"Miss me," I asked her, almost pleading.

"You know I will." She smiled up at me, her eyes shining.

"You guys make me sick," Jewel huffed before

opening the door, making gagging sounds as she bounded down the steps to the limo.

I walked Veronica to the town car, leaning down to give her one last peck before closing the door. "Be good," I told her, and a trickle of laughter filled the air.

Moving aside, I watched and waved at the retreating car. Once it had cleared a block, I pulled out my phone and made my first phone call of the day.

"Tell me you have an answer," I told the person on the other line.

If Veronica knew I'd done a covert operation to find out who this man she would be spending two weeks with, she would probably refuse to talk to me for days. But I convinced myself that I had to know. I had to, even if my conscience told me it was the wrong thing to do. I had to.

In my life, even those who'd told me they loved me had left, time and time again.

DOUBT IN MY MIND

VERONICA

"*H*e'll be fine." Jewel tapped the top of my hands, crossed over my lap, taking my gaze away from outside the plane to her. "You'll see him in two weeks."

I nodded and tried to smile, but I couldn't. Something was off. Levi had never been the clingy kind. He'd been a wonderful boyfriend, perfect to a fault. But he was not clingy.

"You know what will take your mind off things?" Jewel asked, shuffling through her purse and bringing out a pen, handing it to me. "Make a list of things you want to do while we're there."

I opened my mouth, but since what I had in mind was far from what I wanted to say, I pressed my lips together.

"Nica, what's wrong?"

I bit the corner of my lip before saying, "I think Levi's hiding something from me."

Jewel furrowed her brows, tilted her head to one side, then looked sideways. What was it they said about people lying or trying to remember something? Who looked left? And who looked to the right?

"Jewel?" I stuffed my iPad and notebook back in my purse. A loud sound from the airplane engine caused me to jump on my seat. I gripped my armrests, but continued my prodding. "Do you know something?"

"Why would I?" she said quickly. "I barely talk to the guy. You guys are always sucking faces when he's at the office."

That was true. But something niggled at me. I looked away from Jewel and held my hands on my lap again, twisting the belt secured over me. "I can't help but think that what we have is too good to be true. As if something bad is about to happen."

"Why would you say that?"

"I don't know. He's too good for me. He's hot and... he's so hot...and he has money and he can have any girl he wants, but..."

"Geez, Nica. Are you trying to sabotage your own relationship? Haven't you two been through enough crap?"

"We have but..."

"Stop saying but. No buts. I don't want to hear it. What would Chase say if she were here instead of me?" Jewel eyed me ruefully.

I chuckled drily. "She'd say go with my gut. Probably try to convince me to break it off."

"Would she really?"

"No." I shook my head. Chase had expressed her

dislike for Levi but she knew how much I loved him and how happy I was with him. "She'd probably say the same thing. I don't know."

Jewel settled back on her chair. She stayed quiet, deep in thought, for a bit, then said, "He looked worried when we left, yeah, but I think it's probably because he's going to miss you."

"We've been away from each other before."

"Not this long."

"True."

"And not when he doesn't even know where you're going and why...and with whom."

I copied her position, pressing my back on the cushiony seat. "I hate not telling him, but it's work."

"You think if our client wasn't so hot he would still worry?"

"I don't think so, but I would never cheat on him... on anyone."

"He knows that, right?"

"Yeah, of course. I mean...I think so."

Although I was madly in love with Levi, our relationship was still young, fresh. We hadn't been seeing each other for a year yet. We'd had plenty of conversations about life and love, but there were also quite a few things we'd never talked about. Marriage, for one. He's said before that he wasn't against it...but could he see himself with me? Married to me?

Since my previous relationship, with Jake, had ended abruptly and he'd gotten married only a few months later, I'd been a bit wary.

Were my thoughts justified? I didn't honestly know. Was this something I would feel even though I only thought of Levi? And I couldn't think of not being with him?

I thought of all those times in the past when I'd seen him with other women. He'd had a lot of them. If ever I asked about any one of his exes, he was more than willing to answer my questions. He'd always said that the way his relationships ended were mutual, and not one had been serious enough to consider anything beyond dating.

What if he'd one day feel like that about us? He was sweet and attentive and caring.

So then, what was it? Did Levi have a secret? I couldn't even think of what. He'd been honest with me from the start of our relationship. He knew trust was huge for me. I didn't like being blindsided.

A garbled voice came over the plane's speaker telling us that we were ready for take-off and reminding us once again to turn all our cellphones to airplane mode.

Leaning forward, I grabbed my phone out of my purse and sent a lightning-speed message to Levi:

Tu me manques.

He is missing from me. Somehow it was more meaningful than just telling him I loved him.

After switching it to Airplane Mode, I threw my phone back into my purse and settled in my seat, hoping whatever ugly feeling was weighing on me would go away. Levi was with me. He loved me. He'd miss me.

"Everything's fine. He'll be fine. We're fine," I muttered to myself. I bit my bottom lip, tamping down the urge to get up and leave the airplane. Maybe these two weeks away from each other would do us some good. Maybe Jewel was right. It was best I stayed put.

I would hate to ruin my own perfect relationship.

SOUS UN CIEL ÉTOILÉ

LEVI

*T*wo weeks later, I walked alongside Sherri back into the kitchen she'd temporarily commandeered for the night. A special night.

"Good luck, duck," she said, chuckling.

Did I need luck? "I'm prepared." It had taken the entire two weeks to ensure everything was as it should be. I couldn't risk anything going wrong tonight.

Between Chase and myself, we had managed to put together a romantic proposal, *sous un ciel étoilé,* under a canopy of stars. Even the weather had been cooperating so far. It looked like it would be a cloudless, starry night. Money might not buy love and happiness, but it could fund a simple, yet elegant proposal.

In a few hours, Veronica would be arriving from her trip to The Maldives. Chase was going to pick her and Jewel up from the airport, and they'd drive to a restaurant in Sequoia National Park, under the guise of celebrating Lily's current beau's birthday. I had told her

I would be driving from Santa Barbara after checking out a prospective vineyard.

I rode a four-wheeler ATV from the restaurant to the specially picked clearing, where Chase and Maggie were in the middle of arguing how to set up the small square table with a delicate arrangement of wildflowers. Up above on the towering Sequoia trees, Gerard and his husband, Mateo, were securing strings of clear Edison bulbs that would illuminate the secluded spot. Solar-powered luminaries surrounded the table, dotting the ground. About a hundred of the same square lamps were placed along the trail, which would take Veronica to me by a guided horse-ride.

Veronica adored big, romantic gestures.

Once her staff had gotten a whiff of my proposal, they'd all wanted to get involved. The saying *too many cooks in the kitchen spoil the broth* played in my mind constantly.

A vote had been taken earlier by everyone involved in the preparation whether I should propose before dinner or after dessert. The decision was split in the middle, and I would have to leave it to fate. I would know when the right time was.

My phone vibrated as I parked the ATV to the side. Jake sent a text message asking how things were going. I'd received a similar message from Martina that morning. And I replied with a simple "great" to the both of them. It was an understatement. Everything had gone swimmingly, despite a few silly arguments, and I was thrilled to get help from the people who were closest to my (hopefully) future fiancée.

"Chase, shouldn't you start driving to the airport?"

"Nice try, Maggie. The flowers should stay in the middle." Chase moved the wildflower arrangement from where it sat on one side, close to the edge of the table to the middle.

Maggie picked it up and replaced it where it had been. "Side! So Levi can reach across the table to present her the ring!" Maggie extended her hand and flicked it at Chase.

"He's going down on one knee. Aesthetically, the flowers would look better in the middle."

"I have to go down on one knee?" I immediately regretted coming between them. If they were acting like this during the proposal, what horrors would they come up with during the wedding preparations? I assumed Veronica would ask their help. But as always, she had powers to oversee such events, and sort out any foreseeable errors.

I wished she was here now to sort this out. Our communication had been frequent, as she had promised, while she was stuck on the tropical island. I'd felt a tug in my heart when I'd seen how tired Veronica had been throughout the ordeal. There were dark circles under her eyes. She'd looked tanned but not rested. A few times during our Skype calls, I'd watched her get startled by her iPad slamming down on her forehead because she had fallen asleep.

Once I'd been given information regarding who her client was and what he was after, my suspicions had somewhat waned. Although he was a Hollywood celebrity, he was just another man who had fallen hopelessly in love with a woman, and wanted the best for his mate.

I could relate.

A truck came bounding down the trail, and out came Lily and James—her new boyfriend—along with one of the park's senior Rangers. I shook James' proffered hand and hugged Lily. They'd all promised to make themselves scarce once Veronica arrived. In the meantime, they wanted to check out the site.

"Well lookie here, this is some fine work," James said.

"Are you sure you don't want a tent, Levi?" Lily had asked me several times already today.

"Darlin', look at the sky, entirely cloudless. This could never be more perfect. It ain't gonna rain," James informed her, yet again, waving his hands wildly in the air.

Lily pursed her lips, bent down and rubbed her knees. "I'm telling you, it *is* going to rain. I can feel it in my bones." James gave her a smirk. "Oh fine, I'll keep my nose out of it. But I brought an umbrella, just in case." She pivoted and walked back to the other side of the truck.

James shook his head as he laughed. "Women," he muttered, "can't live with them..." I waited for the rest of his statement but nothing followed.

Just as Lily was coming back from the truck with a golf umbrella, Gerard and Mateo descended from the trees. We all stepped back to admire all our work.

Maggie's phone rang and she picked up right away.

"Hello." Then she mouthed "Nica" to us and pointed to her phone.

Veronica was calling her now?

"Hey, Ni--oh...yeah. Uh-huh. Yeah, I'll tell her. I'll handle it. No worries. Okay. Bye."

"What's going on?" Lily and Chase both asked.

Chase took her phone out of her jeans pocket. She read a message on it with a furrow on her forehead. This could not be good...I could feel it in my bones.

"Should I be worried?" I asked as I slid my phone out of my pocket. I couldn't help the slight tremble in my voice.

"She'll be calling you." And as soon as Maggie said it, my phone buzzed in my hand.

"Laurent."

Veronica's voice broke through the static, "Hi, babe."

"Sweetheart, how are you? Are you excited to come home?" *And be back in my arms?* I wanted to add, but all eyes were on me. All ears were too.

"I'm sorry...can't make it...huge storm...crazy wind..." Her words where interrupted with more static, and what could very well be howling winds. "Flight delayed...morning..."

I looked up the clear skies, past the Edison bulbs, and the Sequoia trees. "Your flight is delayed 'til tomorrow morning?"

"Yup. I called Maggie..." she replied. In the background--although I had trouble hearing Veronica--I heard quite an unmistakable man's voice said, "Nica! You're getting wet!"

"Yeah, I know! I'm coming," Veronica yelled back at the man. My hand wrapped around my phone tighter, fighting not to throw it against the large tree trunks. "Sorry, Levi, I have to go. I love—" And all I heard after that was static.

I stared at the screen of my phone until it faded to black. It mocked me. It angered me.

I felt movements around me, and as I lifted my head, Chase walked up to Gerard and Mateo, who nodded and avoided eye contact with me. They headed back up the ladder to take down the lights. Maggie began gathering the luminaries and taking them to James' truck.

Chase caught my attention. Slowly, she made her way to me. "What can you do?" She shrugged. For once, she did seem like she cared about my feelings.

What could I do? I wracked my brain for any solution. One dawned on me. I searched through my contacts and connected with the right person.

I bypassed the pleasantries, and went right to the point, "David, prep the jet. Meet me at the hangar. I'm heading to The Maldives."

"Maldives?" David, my pilot, paused. "I just checked, Levi, there's a tropical storm passing through there right now. Everything's shut down. Couldn't it wait until tomorrow?"

No, it couldn't. I couldn't. "Yeah, I heard that." It would be suicide to go. I felt defeated.

Lily came by my side and rubbed my back, saying under her breath, "She's safe. That's important. She'll be back tomorrow." I hung my head.

"All right." I returned to my phone call. "Don't worry

about it. Good night. I'll call you in the morning if anything changes."

In a matter of minutes, Veronica's friends and family had cleared the area, loading the items on Mateo and James' trucks. With the floral arrangement that was supposed to go on the table propped against her hip, Lily strode up to me. She lifted an arm and squeezed my shoulder.

"Let's just hope she gets back fine," she told me. I cursed myself silently for not thinking that, and for only letting jealousy get hold of me again. "Knowing my daughter, she tried everything she could to get back here on time. She would have wanted to see you tonight, and she would have been ecstatic, cried even, with what you've done. She would have said yes." Lily smiled and patted my arm one more time before heading back to the truck.

"You riding with us?" Mateo asked.

"I'll take the ATV back."

"Are you sure? It's getting dark."

I stared up at the skies again. "Yeah, I'll ride behind you guys. I've got a torch," I informed him. I could tell he wanted to say more, but he decided not to and ambled back to his truck.

As I swung a leg over the four-wheeler seat, I felt a drop on my arm. I let out colorful expletives as the heavens opened up. Lily had been right.

I cursed Mother Nature.

IN HIS ARMS

VERONICA

I was exhausted. My stubbornness against sitting and waiting and letting the storm pass had brought me back to where I wanted to be...twenty-two grueling hours later.

When I arrived at Levi's penthouse, the place was quiet. Too quiet. And there was a chill in the air. I paused by the door to disarm the alarm on the screen and swiped at it with my forefinger, ordering the Smart House to draw the curtains open and let the natural light in. Following that, I tapped on buttons to start a soothing music and ignite the fireplace.

Peace. Comfort. Home. And everything smelled like Levi.

Too exhausted to even charge my phone, I plopped my sore butt on the sofa, placed my head on top of my folded arms, tucked my legs in and drifted off to sleep.

Soon enough, Levi would be home. Soon enough, I would be back in his arms.

I WAS CRADLED in a soft cocoon, a warmth that smelled of nature and the rain. I wished the storm would go away. A steady tattoo swayed me back to sleep. Far too often, the rain would pelt my windows, but this was calming, steady and soothing. Like a beat of one's heart.

That was when I challenged myself to open my heavy eyelids. "It's you."

He might have sensed me stir, might not have heard me. Levi glanced down, and the twinkle in his eye was a revelation of what he wasn't saying out loud. His breath wasn't labored as he walked up the stairs to the second floor of the penthouse, with my legs slung over one of his arms. I reached my hands up and intertwined my fingers behind his neck. I ruffled the ends of his thick, wet hair.

"Where have you been?" I snuggled against his chest, feeling the coolness of his soaked shirt, waiting for his reply.

"I went for a run."

"It's raining," I guessed, burrowing my nose on his chest. Levi and rain. How intoxicating.

"Yes, I got caught in it."

We made it to his bedroom. It was distinctly Levi. Male. Powerful with tiny hints of sweetness and charm. Dangerous in all aspects, particularly for a weak heart like mine.

He laid me on top of the bed. My body arched against the silken sheets as I reached for him. "Don't go.

Stay. I missed you." A pout hinted on my lips. He kissed it away.

"I missed you too, more than you could ever know. But I have to change out of my wet clothes and shower."

"Take me." With a slight pull of my hand, his head bowed back to me, and Levi let me know just how much he did miss me. His kiss was deep, urgent, and desperate, almost telling me I'd been gone far too long.

"Bath sound good?"

"It sounds perfect." My man was great at many things, one of which was throwing me deliriously fantastic baths. He picked me up again and padded to the en suite bathroom.

From my vantage point atop the marble vanity, I watched as Levi uncorked bottles and poured liquids into the hot water. I admired how his muscles stretched and flexed under his wet white t-shirt. His running shorts grabbed onto his buttocks too, and when he bent over to test the water, I delighted in my view.

"Bath's ready." Levi kissed the edge of my right collarbone, peeking out from under my champagne-colored blouse. He thumbed the pearls against the skin of my neck. "Can we leave these on?"

I smiled, shyly, blushed and nodded. Levi took that as a cue to undress me, one button at a time, one stocking at a time. A zip undone. A clasp unsnapped. Each moment created a mounting desire, a fire in my belly. Every movement was punctuated with a kiss, a caress. A touch. A shiver. A spark.

He guided me to the tub, large enough to fit us both.

It faced an expansive window, which opened up to the glorious view of the Golden Gate Bridge at dusk after the rain. He added the melodic voice of a man and his guitar to the sound system. With the light lowered, Levi lit several candles in the room. The water with its concoction of essential oils, bath salts and bubbles was something the doctor ordered, after a long trip home. I dipped my feet in one at a time, letting my body adjust to the temperature.

Once I was covered in bubbles, Levi stepped back, admiration and desire in his eyes, and peeled off his clothes. Taking his time, he delighted in the little gasps that made their way out of my mouth. He kissed my forehead, letting his lips linger before I moved forward and made room for him behind me.

I leaned my head against him, and lifted our hands together from the bubbles and the water, and intertwined our fingers. "Why didn't you run indoors? Didn't you check the weather before you left?"

He sighed. The warmth of his breath tickled my skin. "I can't trust the weather reports these days. Can't even trust the skies."

"Hmmm..." His lips made their way behind my ear, nibbling at the sensitive spot, and stroking the skin underneath my pearl necklace. My eyes rolled to the back of my head. This man could make my toes curl with the simplest of touches.

How could I have thought that our relationship was in danger before I left?

"I'm happy you're back. I was going crazy without

you. That's why I went for a run outside. To get some fresh air, make me think better."

"Did it work?"

Levi massaged the ache on my shoulders, created by hours of lugging my bags and pulling on my suitcase, and sleeping on pillows that hadn't belonged to me, and hadn't smelled of his scent.

"All I know is that the rain isn't too bad. It is somewhat an omen of good things to come."

"And Mother Nature isn't quite a bitch," I added.

"Yes, that too." He chuckled at a joke I had a feeling I wasn't privy to, but I didn't mind. We could laugh about it later. "What kind of good things are you expecting?"

I ran my hands on his legs, lightly scraping my nails on his warm skin, earning a small growl of appreciation from Levi. He reciprocated by ghosting his fingers over my shoulders, down my chest, until his hands disappeared beyond the bubbles.

"For instance, it rained the first time I met you," he spoke against the side of my cheek. I turned my head to meet his lips.

"Did it?" I managed to mutter against his mouth.

"Yes."

"Remind me again?" I asked, but my heart wasn't completely in it. I could only think of what he was doing to me with his hands and lips, and how my body responded.

"Later," Levi said, as he helped me turn around to face him, my legs astride his. Lifting the pearls off my neck with his thumb, he found the pulse on my neck and licked it, and my head lolled back to give him more access.

In a tone that made me lose all my inhibitions, Levi whispered, "I promise."

LA DÉESEE DE L'AMOUR

LEVI

I trailed my fingers over the contours of her right hip and waist, watching goose bumps rise, scattering like minuscule nodules of fire. A fire that set my own desires aflame. Veronica hummed against my neck, and my arousal heightened.

Two weeks without her had been far too long and lonely. Now that she was back in my arms, I had no intentions of letting her go again. Ever.

She stretched against me.

"You're teasing me," I growled in her ear, pressing her body to mine as I let my fingers grasp her bottom.

A knowing smile was her reply. Her hands stroked my chest, one going up and the other going down. My back was pushed into the sheets as Veronica lifted herself up and straddled my lap, circling her hips against me. The sateen sheets fell off and left her exposed.

Hands roved from her stomach to her chest. Hands

that looked peculiar, yet, familiar. Hands that didn't belong to me.

From the threshold of a bedroom fashioned to look like a scene in a tropical resort, I watched, appalled and horrified at the sight of a man who was making Veronica moan in pleasure.

"Veronica?" My voice faltered.

She tilted her head and looked over her shoulder, the springs of the mattress creaking beneath her as her body bounced. "I couldn't help it, Levi. I was lonely."

The man sat up, grabbing her hair, making her arch her body to him. I couldn't see his face as it disappeared between her breasts, but his mockery was clear as the blue skies. "You should have married her when you had the chance."

The color red exploded in my mind. I lunged forward, with my sight blurred, my hands fisted, and my heart shattered.

I woke gasping for air, my hands balled up the sheets underneath me. Blinking my eyes to see clearer, I realized I was back in my own bedroom, shaking and soaked in my own sweat. I looked to my side and saw Veronica curled on her side of the bed. *Breathe*, I told myself. It was just a horrid dream.

In that moment, I wanted to reach out to Veronica and hold her in my arms. But something was suffocating me. Remnants of the anger I had felt in dream state spilled into my reality. I needed to get a grip before I touched her. I rolled off the bed and dressed for another outdoor run.

❧

"You haven't told me how your trip went."

She picked up another piece of chocolate-drizzled crepe off her plate and lifted it to her mouth. "I was busy," she said, shrugging one shoulder, when she finished chewing, and offered me another piece.

"Did you like the Maldives?" I stared right into her eyes, twinkling with her smile, as I wrapped my lips around the fork. Yes, I could, beyond any doubt, spend the rest of my life with this goddess.

Veronica hummed, then nodded. A drop of whipped cream fell on top of one of her breasts. As helpful as I ever was, I licked her clean.

"Sweet." The word was meant, not for the cream, but the taste of her skin. "Would you like to go back someday?"

"I'm going back in November for the actual event."

"Oh?" I hadn't thought of that. "With me?" I asked, my voice low and serious.

She smiled and nodded, licking off cream from the fork. "I would love that. Maybe I'd be able to actually enjoy the sun and the beach."

"I wouldn't be too sure of that." I gave her bottom a little squeeze.

Veronica laid her head on my chest. "I missed you so much. It was so hard to be away from you."

Brushing off her hair to the side, I kissed her forehead and asked, "Why don't we go away this weekend?"

"To Maldives?"

"Or somewhere closer." Somewhere where tropical storms, or any storms of any kind, could not hamper my plans. "We can go to Napa. Finally see the vineyard?"

She hummed, circling her finger over the tip of my clavicle. "There's work…"

I didn't let her finish. "You can work from there. The house has Wi-Fi."

"I know that. But…" She pushed up to face me, cradling my head in her hands. "I've just returned. I have to meet with clients."

"Conference call. Skype. FaceTime." Something had to work. She had to agree.

"And I have to go back to my apartment."

"I watered all your plants. Your orchid has three blooms."

Veronica leaned forward and planted a kiss on my lips. "Okay. Let's leave today."

I chuckled. "We can't today. You promised Sandrine you won't miss tonight's dinner since you didn't make the last one."

"Right. I should tell Chase that I'm leaving again. She is *not* going to like me."

Threading my fingers through her hair, I brought her forehead closer to press on mine. "How can anyone not like you? You're perfect in every way.

"You're just saying that because I'm naked on top of you."

"Yes, you are." Inhaling deeply, I basked in the sweet aroma of her skin. "We have time before dinner."

MANAGING to arrive on time by the skin of our teeth, Veronica dashed up the steps of Jake and Sandrine's Pacific Heights home, with me lagging behind.

"Relax. They won't start without us. And I'm not too keen on trying out anything Jake has prepared," I told her as she waited for me by the door.

"I don't like being late. You know that."

A lock of rich brown hair sprang from her braid, which cascaded over her right shoulder. Her enticing, flawless, smooth-as-silk shoulder. I found myself leaning down and pressing my lips to it. "It was your fault, you know. If you hadn't seduced me..."

"It was so not my fault. And behave." She playfully patted the side of my face before pressing the doorbell.

My lips moved up to the crook of her neck. "Why should I?"

Her breathing became irregular. "Sandrine said...they have other...guests," Veronica said between pants.

"It's just Nati."

"Natalie's in town?" She pulled away from me so quickly that I almost fell forward.

"Yeah. And her boyfriend. What's his name?"

"Diego?"

"That one. Have you met him before? Nice bloke. Friendly."

Veronica sucked in her bottom lip. Had I missed something? Perhaps Veronica was uncomfortable around Natalie, given my past with her. I was about to put her mind at ease on the matter when the door in front of us opened.

LE TEMPS DU PERDU

*I*nstead of being greeted by one of the people we expected, we faced Chase. This dinner would be more interesting than I'd originally thought. If Chase couldn't stand me, she had stronger animosity toward Jake, and it bewildered me to see her in Jake's home, standing in all her leathers, paired with her dark mood, with a goblet of red wine in her hand. At least, I hoped it was red wine and not blood.

"Oh my goodness! Chase!" Veronica swung her arms around her friend, who grinned at her and sneered at me. "I didn't know you're going to be here."

Chase pulled Veronica in and I followed along. Chase handed the wine glass to Veronica, who accepted and sipped.

"Natalie was in class this morning, and she told me about tonight. I haven't seen you since you came back, because someone has been too selfish to share—" Chase flicked an unimpressed glance over her shoulder to me.

"—so she asked Sandrine if I could come, and here I am."

Veronica leaned her head on her friend's upper arm as she hugged her closer. "Aw, I missed you too. I had to get some rest after the trip. Sorry."

"Like you got any rest." She sent me another seething look, to which I merrily replied with a smug look.

"They're here! Jacob!" I heard Sandrine from inside the kitchen. And I could smell something a bit off too. Jake's cooking. He had been horrible cook in university, and judging by the smell coming from his kitchen, he hadn't improved.

Sandrine, wearing a blue dress, which cinched above her waist and showed off her round belly, darted toward Veronica and wrapped her in her arms before giving her cheeks kisses. It was clear I wasn't the only who had missed her. Jake followed Sandrine.

"My, my, you've grown since last I saw you, Sandrine," Veronica quipped. "May I?" Her hand hovered over Sandrine's middle. Veronica glanced up, and our eyes met.

There was a glint in her eyes. A hope that maybe someday we could feel the same happiness that our friends shared.

"I'm humongous!" Sandrine complained.

"Sandrine," Veronica started, "You look beautiful. I'd have a bigger belly than that if I ate too many donuts." Right then, I imagined Veronica pregnant with my child.

"Can you give us a hand?" Jake broke through my thoughts. "I have guinea fowl in the oven."

"Guinea fowl? Whatever possessed you to make that?" He could barely cook eggs.

Jake wiped his hand on his face in frustration. "My very pregnant wife asked for it."

Natalie came in, quietly laughing at whatever her new boyfriend must have said. It was good to see her happy. I gave her a quick wave and turned to inspect dinner. I glared at Jake. The man should never be allowed inside a kitchen. He'd give Lily Stewart a run for her money when it came to world's worst cook. I would need to have a talk with my cousin. Pregnant or not, she wouldn't be getting what she was craving. The guinea fowl did not survive.

❧

KITCHEN DUTY BECAME MINE. I didn't mind much. Dinner was saved, many thanks to preparedness of Jake and Sandrine's housekeeper, Mara. She had stocked up on other ingredients. Maybe she'd tasted Jake's cooking too. And if she had, the poor woman deserved a raise.

Surprisingly, Diego was rather knowledgeable in the kitchen as well. While the rest of our group gathered around the cheese plate, he made a side salad for the chicken dish I had prepared. We worked quietly and efficiently, occupying either side of the room, and staving off Jake's continual offers to lend a hand.

We all listened to Veronica's tales of woe during her flight back home from The Maldives, leaving out the details of the actual trip and her client's identity. Sandrine and Jake couldn't stop gushing over their plans for after the baby was born. Nati and Chase talked about the new workout classes Diego offered to those who were willing to take them. "Less tortuous" as Chase explained to Veronica, who only said that she would think about it. I could think of other ways to keep her fit.

I kept quiet the entire time, loving the easy conversation that flowed at the table. Endless laughter, and comfort, and warmth.

Diego offered to help with the cleanup.

"Thanks for the help again." I'd poured two fingers of scotch in two glasses for me and him— we deserved as much.

"Think nothing of it. Nati told me that the cooking might not be successful." Diego said this in a lowered voice.

As soon as her name was mentioned, Nati came around and hugged Diego from behind. "Isn't he great?" she asked me, with her left cheek pressed on his wide back.

Her engagement ring flickered under the overhead lights in the kitchen. As fast as things had progressed between Nati and Diego, I was excited for the two of them. They'd announced their engagement and pregnancy right after dinner. I raised my glass to them both.

"And to think, we owe it all to Nica." Nati smiled at Diego.

"Veronica? My Veronica?" I wiped my hands on a kitchen towel, and then placed one on my chest.

"Yeah. She didn't tell you? It was a funny story,

really." Nati and Diego gazed into each other's eyes while she continued, "Imagine if their date had gone better—"

"Who went on a date? You dated Veronica?" I pointed an accusatory finger at Diego.

"Yes." His smile widened, rows of white teeth flashed. I clenched my jaw. "You don't remember meeting me?"

"Relax, Levi. They went on one date," Nati reasoned, while Diego surreptitiously urged her behind his muscular frame.

Where did they go? How long ago was this? Did they kiss? Did they sleep together? Where was I when all of these happened?

"When was this? Why didn't I know this?" My jaw clicked as I clenched it harder.

"Calm down. It's nothing to stress over." Diego raised one hand in front of him.

Jake came in, followed by the rest of them.

My eyes caught Veronica's immediately. "I am calm," I said through gritted teeth.

Jake came to my side and placed an arm between Diego and me. "Why don't we step outside for a moment? Get some fresh air. Fresh perspective?"

I had made a mess of things in a blink of an eye. And I didn't know how to fix it.

Rubbing a hand over my face, I sucked in a deep breath and followed them to the terrace.

"You still don't remember when we first met?" Diego asked in his baritone voice once we stepped out into the cool night.

"I don't know what you're talking about," I told him and turned to Jake, who shrugged.

"The cake tasting? You were with a woman. With the..." He circled his hands over his chest. "And I came in late?"

The cake tasting. How could I have forgotten? "Of course. You came out to talk to me after..."

"After you were kneed in the balls."

"You were what?" Jake asked.

I groaned, rubbing my palm over my eyes. I messed things up then too. "That was a nightmare. She had bony knees." Because I couldn't think of anything else to say or do, I laughed.

"She was something. Gave that spoon a good licking," Diego added with a chuckle.

"I'm confused. What's going on?" Jake asked again.

"It's nothing. I'll tell you another day." I waved a hand at Jake. "I'm sorry for how I reacted. It's been a trying few days."

Diego looked over his shoulder. "I heard you're taking the big leap. Nica is quite the girl."

"So is Natalie... She did tell you we were...?"

Diego nodded. "She and I have no secrets. You can't start a relationship that way. It would never succeed."

My steps faltered as I thought of what I'd never told Nica. Discussion about my family was rare. I'd only spoken about Martina. I didn't offer much about my family's past. My secrets weren't for the faint of heart. And I was afraid that it would be too much for her to handle. They were too damning.

I couldn't tell her. I would try my hardest to make sure she'd never find out.

❧

THE DRIVE BACK WAS QUIET.

"I want to go to my apartment," Veronica said while we were at a stop. Her voice was firm. She was looking straight ahead.

A grunt came out of my mouth instead of an apology or an explanation.

Like a good boyfriend, I did what I was told. I brought her home. She had left her luggage and bags in the penthouse, so she would be back. I hoped. She had only brought a small purse with her to dinner.

Veronica did not wait for me to open her door. Even before I completed parking, her seatbelt was off, and one of her feet was already on the ground. Although she didn't slam the passenger door, it felt like she had. It would have been better if she had. All she did was walk quietly to her door, and without a glance back, she unlocked it and walked into her apartment.

That voice in my head, from my dream mocked me. *You should have married her when you had the chance.*

Had I lost my chance again?

SOUS UN BEAU CEIL BLEU

"*Il était têtu et refusiat d'admettre qu'il avait tort,*" Martina had told my father about me years ago, when I was about seven. Martina was right. I was stubborn and refused to admit that I was wrong.

If Veronica were any other woman, I'd turn around and think 'good riddance'. If she were any other woman, I wouldn't have cared if she had dated half the city before me. As far as I knew, Veronica had been in two other relationships before Jake. She had been honest about those, but we had never broached the casual dating scenarios. Part of that was the fact that I didn't want to give her my *number*. The number of women I'd been with. I had been thankful she had never asked. She'd asked about some of my dalliances, and I'd been fine answering a few questions if only to keep her from asking more.

Was it my own guilt? My conscience coming at me?

My outburst in Jake's kitchen had angered her more than I expected. It didn't matter that I'd straightened it out with Diego.

I gripped the steering wheel and thrashed inside my car. I could use a run right now to clear my head, think of what I needed to say. Or there had to be a flower shop open at this late hour. Or I could simply go inside the apartment with the key she had given me and talk to her. Looking at my phone one more time, I realized that I'd been sitting in the car for an hour, and I still hadn't found the right solution.

What if there wasn't a right solution? I could sit for another hour and come up with the best ideas to apologize, but what if all she wanted was for me to admit that I was wrong?

With uncertainty, I unfolded myself out of the car, locked it and proceeded to her door. I lifted my hand to knock, but her key seared itself to my palm. I unlocked the door instead and stepped inside.

My heart broke at the sight that met me.

Veronica sat on her floor, hugging her knees against her body, just a few steps from the entrance. Her head was down, her hair spilling over her shoulders. A sob echoed in the room.

I went to her and wrapped her in my arms. Her body shifted toward me, her fingers clawing at the back of my shirt as I picked her up and took her to the sofa.

The words "I'm sorry" were whispered in the air. We said them in unison.

I lay on my back and she curled on top of me. Her hair felt like silk in my hands. Her tears soaked my shirt. I lifted her head up so I could see what I had caused, burn that in my mind, and remember never to cause her the same sadness again. Her sob met my lips.

"I was wrong to react that way. I shouldn't have. You had the right to date--"

"No, I was wrong. I should have told you. Diego and I went out just once before the cake tasting."

"You were allowed to date anyone." It pained me to say it out loud.

"At the time, I wasn't too sure. I thought I'd give it a try. With all the crap that was happening, it seemed like a good idea. You know what's funny?" I hummed. "We mostly talked about you." Veronica tried to push up and sit, but all I wanted was to hold her closer. "I'm getting mascara all over your shirt."

"It doesn't matter." I caressed her cheeks and tucked her hair behind her ears. With my thumbs, I erased the dark lines on her face. With my kisses, I hoped to erase the memory of those tears.

She snuggled her head back under my chin. I could feel her heart marching to the same beat as mine. Then she proceeded to tell me how she came to have dinner with Diego, to test the dating waters once again after her break up with Jake. And why he showed up to the cake tasting—an idea concocted by Chase to save Veronica when I brought someone who shouldn't have been there in the first place, and while Veronica herself wasn't certain about her feelings with me.

Diego could have made Veronica very happy. And perhaps that was where my insecurities lay. I wasn't a perfect man, but would I be able to convince Veronica that I was perfect for her?

"He met Natalie later. It was a chance encounter," she continued to explain.

"And now they're getting married and having a baby."

"I know. Isn't that crazy?"

I couldn't answer. Not when I wanted to share the same significant, life-changing events with her. I murmured sweet nothings into her ear as I threaded her long hair through my fingers. I kissed every part of her until we laid our insecurities to rest. At least for the night.

❦

VERONICA HADN'T STOPPED LAUGHING or smiling since we hit the road. The colorful Pucci scarf I'd given her when we were in Paris last year for Jake and Sandrine's wedding preparations matched her countenance. Even with the dark sunglasses on, I knew her eyes were twinkling. She was high on life, and I couldn't help but be happy with her. It made the drive to the vineyard much more exciting.

I was over the moon. The Napa Valley vineyard, *Casa de Marysol*, was my pride and joy, much like Bliss Events was to Veronica. Finally, after several months, I would be able to show Veronica my 'baby'. An old friend of Martina's, Santiago de la Cruz, had told me the troubles the proprietors had gone through with their only child suffering and dying of a rare cancer the previous year.

After a few visits, and tasting the wine they had produced, I was convinced that I could raise it from the ashes, so to speak. And I had. Our sparkling wine was up against the internationally favored Chateau du Laurent's own *cuvée*. Of course, none of it would have been possible if I hadn't met Veronica, and on that same fateful night, decided to turn my life around.

We had hit a few snags, but the vineyard's previous owners had refused to give up. With their help, a few visits from Santiago, and simple hints from Martina, *Casa de Marysol* had survived the worst of it, so far. It was named after the previous owners' late daughter.

Veronica looked around in quiet awe, with her hand over her lips and her sunglasses pushed up over her head. She'd had uncertainties about the difference in our wealth and statuses before; I hoped this wouldn't bring those fears back.

What I wanted her to see were the possibilities—of visiting the vineyard together, as much as we could. Of our future children running through the grounds. Our friends and family, dining with us under the moonlight on the terrace. Making love on the balcony underneath the stars.

I reached over and wrapped her hand in mine, kissing the tips of her fingers. "What do you think?"

Her grin spread from one ear to the other. "What do I think? It's gorgeous. You never told me how beautiful this place is. You've had events here before?"

I laughed. My Veronica, ever the planner. "Yes, I have."

Clem and Adel Lotta met us at the front of main

house with Adel's older sister, Anita. Their tanned skin showed that they had been working hard under the sun, but their genuine smiles told me they were happy to do so. I introduced Veronica to the people who were close enough to be called my family. Whenever I spoke of *Casa de Marysol*, I made sure to mention the roles they played in its success, and in a way, in my own personal growth. Veronica was welcomed with opened arms.

Adel led her inside, an arm around Veronica's waist. Clem trailed behind, talking as much as Adel was. Anita hooked her hand around my elbow. "It's nice to see her finally make it. I was nervous there for you. I didn't think you could do it." Anita was as close to an aunt as I could get.

"Why doesn't anyone believe I can make things happen?" I said with a laugh. "Is everything ready?"

She smiled and squeezed my arm. "I can't believe you would even ask that. Of course everything is set. You just settle for a while, give her a quick tour of the house, and invite her out for lunch. Then you do what you came here to do."

I kissed the top of Anita's head, which only reached to my shoulders. "Thank you. The skies are clear today. Cloudless. No sign of rain." I winked. Anita lifted her hand and crossed her fingers.

I took over from Adel and carried a giggling Veronica up the stairs, straight to the bedroom we would be sharing. Light spilled inside the large room through the floor-to-ceiling windows that made up one wall, and the door that led out to the balcony, which looked over the spread of the land. A luxurious king-size canopy bed occupied a quarter of the space, and that's where I laid Veronica.

"Aren't you supposed to show me around?" She giggled between the words, while I ran my hands over her ribs, pushing up her shirt, and licked around her navel.

"Shhh… I'm doing my own explorations right now." I produced another giggle from her as I undid her jeans button, and blew hot breath along the top seam of her lace panties.

She moaned as I went farther down. Her hands snaked from my shoulders and threaded through my hair. "Levi." My name came out in a sigh.

After ridding her of her jeans, I gazed up and found her eyes, eager and willing. "I'm so happy you're here."

"I am too." Propping herself on her elbows, she offered me a sweet smile.

I returned to my intentions of having dessert before lunch, nipping at the curve of her hips, which led me to the sensitive skin of her thighs. I intended to make her scream my name as her stomach shook in ecstasy and her toes curled in delight. And after this, I intended to ask her *the* question and receive the answer that would make me the happiest man in the world.

❧

VERONICA FELT WARM AGAINST ME. Our bodies were slicked with sweat, but neither of us cared to move. I could stay in this bed with her for all eternity. But her belly grumbled, and I was all too aware of what I was keeping her, and myself, from.

"You must be hungry. I didn't mean to take forever." I pushed up and rolled her on her back.

"I'm always hungry. And you always take forever." She pulled on the sheet to cover her naked body.

I kissed the crook of her neck. "You've never complained before."

Veronica threaded her fingers behind my neck, and I stared right into her eyes. "I'm not complaining now."

"We better get up and eat. Picnic lunch okay with you?"

"A picnic? How romantic."

I offered my hand and helped her up from the bed.

If she only knew how romantic I planned to be. I picked my clothes off the floor and noticed my phone vibrating on the night table. Any other time I would have ignored it. Everyone knew I'd be spending time with Veronica, and I didn't like being interrupted when I was with her, particularly today. But something prickled the back of my neck. That prickle intensified when I saw the name on my screen.

I snatched my phone up and answered, "Laurent."

"Olivier," Sandrine's father, François, quietly said, "*Votre grand-mère.*"

"Martina?" I choked out her name.

"*Oui, reviens à la maison.*" His voice shook as he asked me to return home. To France.

As I stood there, François informed me how my grandmother had been found unconscious in her bedroom, that doctors were running tests, while she laid in a hospital bed in a coma. I promised François I would return to France immediately. There was no question about it.

"Levi? What's wrong?" Veronica walked over to me as I sat back on the bed, weakened from the news.

I looked at her but I couldn't see beyond the fog in my mind. "Martina is in a coma. They think she had a stroke. I have to go."

She nodded, tears ready to spill out of her eyes. "Of course."

I was wasting time sitting on my ass. I dialed David's number and ordered him to get the private plane ready. Then I asked him to call his brother to come pick me up. That hour drive to the hangar in San Francisco would take too long. A 'copter ride would be faster.

As soon as we found the Lottas, I gave them the news. Everyone hugged me one by one, although I had a difficult time determining who said what.

"We'll take Veronica back to the city," Clem informed me.

Veronica. I stared at her red-rimmed eyes, the fingers that she kept twisting, and her lips, still plump from my kisses. "Come with me." I reached out for her hand.

"Of course I'll go. I'll tell Chase." She leaned her head on my chest and kissed the hands that held hers.

She would be there for me.

Á PARIS

"*A*nything to drink, sir?" my attendant asked. Her predecessor, and my friend, Sophie had just given birth to a lovely little girl. I hadn't yet remembered what the new girl's name was, the attendant's. Sophie's girl was called Amélie.

Tonight wasn't the right time to get acquainted. I glanced at her briefly and muttered "No thanks." She nodded and let me be. I held my phone, ready to jump at any call or message.

"Levi." Jake sat beside me, clapping a hand on my shoulder to get my attention. "Sandrine spoke to the doctor in charge. The specialist she sent arrived a few minutes ago..." His words were interrupted by my phone ringing.

I didn't hesitate to answer, "Laurent.

The man on the other line introduced himself as Gerd Ladouceur, a friend of Sandrine's and a cardiologist. Martina was awake, and she would be kept

109

under close observation for the next few days. He also added that Martina had yelled at the staff for keeping her in bed when there was work to be done.

I couldn't help but wonder, what if no one had found her? What if Martina had been at the chateau in Bordeaux, where all her employees were busy in the field, rather than her house in Paris?

I should have been there.

What had she been doing in Paris in the first place? She avoided the capital city at all costs, especially when my mother was around. And I'd heard that my mother was busy painting the town all shades of red.

I didn't realize Jake had stayed beside me until he tapped my shoulder. "It seems Martina is awake and making threats now," I told him. His shoulders visibly relaxed. "Where are Sandrine and Veronica?"

"They're in the room, looking at baby clothes online." He rubbed his tired eyes and stifled a yawn.

I nodded at Jake. I hadn't expected them to come, but when Veronica and I had arrived at the hangar, they'd been waiting.

Like Jake had said, they were in the bedroom at the back of the aircraft. But the two women weren't looking at baby items, they were quietly talking. Their murmurs stopped as soon as they heard me enter.

"Hey, love," Veronica smiled, but worry filled her eyes.

"I'm going to see Jacob," Sandrine excused herself, sitting up carefully with her hand supporting her belly. She pressed a kiss on my cheek before leaving the room.

I propped my head on a pillow on the bed and

reached out for Veronica. She wrapped an arm around me, stretching her body against mine. Just having her beside me calmed my nerves. How did I live my life before I had her?

"She's awake now," I said after kissing her forehead.

"That's good, right?"

"I think so. She's already making the hospital staff shake in their shoes. She hates hospitals."

"I hate them too," she confessed.

I hugged her tighter, squeezing her shoulder with one hand. "Why is that?"

"When my dad was dying, Mom and I spent a lot of time in hospitals. The nurses were nice to me, but *nice* couldn't save my dad." Veronica released a shaky exhale.

"Did he suffer?"

"The nurses said he didn't. He was on a lot of morphine at the end. Even at a young age, I knew what they were doing." My heart constricted for the young Veronica and for the woman that I held in my arms now. "How about your father?"

And this was it—the time I'd been dreading. I pressed my lips into a straight line before replying, "I don't know. I didn't see him." The pain of his sudden death and the memory of his once strong self should have filled my mind. But I'd severed my relationship with him long before he passed. If I told Veronica, she would ask more questions, and those questions would lead to a past I didn't want surfacing. Not now. Not ever. "I wasn't told until three days later, the day of his funeral." My jaw clenched, feeling that powerful anger which had shrouded me for years but which I had tried to ignore.

Veronica tilted her head up. I refused to meet her gaze. I worked my jaw with a hand as I continued, "He was with his mistress. I don't know which one. There had been a lot of them." Like father, like son, my mother used to say. "I think if Martina hadn't forced my mother, she would have kept it from me much longer. There was no love lost between my parents." And no love lost between me and Lucinde, my mother.

She hadn't told me about his death, because she hadn't thought my father deserved to be mourned.

"I'm sorry." Veronica rubbed my five o'clock shadow with her knuckles. I pushed her hand up across my lips.

"I'm just glad you're here with me. I didn't know how much it meant to have someone like you at a time like this."

❧

AS SOON AS WE DISEMBARKED, we were greeted by Martina's chauffeur. I shook my head. Martina already knew I was coming and was trying to take care of me. The driver informed us that she had muscled her way out of the hospital and forced Gerd to let her go home. I didn't know how she'd done it. I just knew she could.

The four of us rode in silence. Sandrine was out of the car before any of us, even with her growing stomach, and Jake followed faithfully. I held Veronica's hand as we entered Martina's mansion. We were all exhausted from the tension and the flight, but Veronica stood strong beside me. I gripped her hand as we faced the curved stairs that would lead me to Martina's chambers. Veronica tugged back.

Her face was somber when I looked over. "Go in without me. It's your grandmother."

"It's fine. You can come." I pressed my lips into a thin line, and my chest constricted.

She shook her head. "Let her see you, and only you. I can meet her later." I saw determination in her eyes. I was too tired to argue, especially knowing I wouldn't win.

I leaned in for a deep kiss before leaving her at the bottom of the stairs. I'd asked her to wait comfortably in one of the salons. Martina's servants would be around to see to her needs.

&

MARTINA PURSED HER LIPS. "I'm fine."

She wasn't fine. She looked pallid and weak under the bleak lighting. Machines beeped beside her, wires and tubes stuck out between her and whatever Gerd had set up in her bedroom.

"You were in a coma, Onna." I kept my voice steady, but my hands shook over my knees as I sat on the edge of her bed. "You should have stayed at the hospital."

She scoffed. "It was unnecessary. The doctor said so himself. I was just tired." She waved her hand in the air. Her words slurred a little but she tried hard to not make it obvious.

It was difficult to not show my frustration. I rubbed

my temples, waiting for my breathing to slow. "What are you doing here? In Paris? Didn't you have a harvest to watch over?"

Martina leaned against her headboard and averted her eyes. The stubborn line on her lips showed, even with the faint lighting in her room.

"Tell me, or I'll start digging. I'll find out sooner or la—"

"Alexandre is back."

And that was all she had to say. The words carried a lot more meaning.

"When?"

"Last week."

"Why?"

"Reasons."

I chuckled without mirth and shook my head. "Where is he now?"

Martina huffed out a heavy breath. "I don't know. Ask your mother." Martina raised an eyebrow as she said 'mother', as though it were the vilest word.

It was my turn to scoff. These were two people who would hate to see me more than I would hate to see them. Lucinde and Alexandre. "That's never going to happen. And he wouldn't go to her. We both know that."

"He'll turn up soon."

"Is that why you had..." I waved my hand at her frail body, covered by piles of sheets and a duvet.

She shook her head.

"Somehow I don't believe you."

"You're going to believe what you choose to believe.

You're as hard-headed as your father ever was," she stated.

"He was as hard-headed as his mother," I fired back. She narrowed her eyes at me.

Martina was right, though. Alexandre would turn up again soon, and I wouldn't want to be around when he did. I stood and sauntered toward the door.

"Leaving already?" For a moment, she actually sounded tired and fragile, very unlike Martina.

I squeezed the bridge of my nose and closed my eyes. "I brought Veronica."

Martina pushed herself up, groaning. "She's here?" I sent her a warning look. "Don't give me that look. Ask her to come up. I'd like to meet her."

"No," I said firmly.

"Why are you so afraid? Of all the people in the city at this moment, I am the least of your worries." It was hard to admit it, but once again, she was right.

"Fine." I conceded. "She's been eager to meet you too. Just don't—"

She stopped me with a raised hand. "My lips are sealed."

"Thank you. You'd better brush your hair, make yourself presentable. I wouldn't want her to think you've gone senile." A smile twitched at a corner of my mouth.

Martina tutted. "I happen to know I look better than most forty year olds out there, even after waking up from a coma." With an air of superiority she ordered me, "Bring her up. I want to see this woman who has you wriggling like a worm."

A PARISIAN NIGHT

VERONICA

$\mathcal{M}$y heart slammed against my chest, and my pulse drummed inside my head. I inhaled, staring at my reflection in the full-length mirror, as I stood in a glittery dress that cost more than I could afford in a lifetime.

The curls on top of my head were piled artfully by a professional who had come in and pulled, poked and prodded at my scalp, and added a jewel-studded comb, which could possibly be older than me. Another stylist took over, and her job was to make my skin shine and sparkle like it was natural to do so. She had helped me slip into the vintage couture dress I had on now, paired with exorbitantly-priced shoes.

Neither of them introduced themselves. They came in to do their duties as they were hired and paid to do.

I touched the brilliance that hung from my ears and those that covered my décolletage. Drops of diamonds, shining against my warm skin.

"You're a vision," a voice startled me from behind.

"Martina." Her hair was done in an old-fashioned chignon. Her long dress swooshed around her as she ambled to me with a slight limp.

"No wonder Levi is so in awe of you." The *mater de familia* smoothed a hand over one of my cheeks. Her voice was soothing, with only a slight French accent. The only sign of her stroke was a mild weakness on one corner of her lips.

"Thank you so much for all this." I waved my hands over my hair, the dress, and my beautiful surroundings.

Martina tilted her head and regarded me the same way she had the moment we had met, like I were some curious thing. Maybe I was. I felt out of sorts in this world. I'd had trouble with the language, and found it difficult to communicate with the people who constantly attended to me. The room I had occupied for the past three days was bigger than my own apartment, and had a magical view of the sprawling gardens.

If fairy tales existed, I was in one. But I was no princess, I was a troll who pretended to be royalty. I was like Shrek, but less green, less grumpy, and all awkward.

"Why don't we head downstairs and you can meet our guests?"

The past three days, I had berated myself for not remembering when Levi's birthday was. It was basic girlfriend knowledge and for Pete's sake, I'm an event planner! It had been highlighted, underlined, boldfaced in my calendar for months! I had even picked the perfect present for him, a limited edition watch that I had saved for, for months. A watch that was sitting

117

inside my dresser drawer, gift-wrapped in shiny silver paper.

I had panicked over the phone with Chase after meeting Martina, when Levi's grandmother had informed me that it would be the perfect time to throw him a birthday party. Chase had promptly ordered me to stop beating myself over it, that I'd been under a lot of stress, and even the most prepared person would forget, given the situation. She'd said I should just enjoy the following days amongst Paris royalty.

Martina had been kind, and far too attentive for someone who should have been resting. The night we'd met, I'd been so nervous that, as I'd hugged her, I managed to pull one of the wires from her machine and sent it beeping loudly in her bedroom. It had been a solid ice breaker though, as she had laughed it off (Levi hadn't). I'd made myself scarce every time the doctors, including Jake and Sandrine, had come to check on her. She'd sought me, time after time afterwards, to tell me the nitty-gritty information she'd received, and huffed at.

"What do these young doctors know? Do I look like I'm some old wilt to you, Veronica?" she had asked me once, to which I had adamantly shook my head. "Exactly! You can see it. I can see it. Why can't they see it? And Olivier, the worst of them all." She had pouted, and then she'd waved it off and asked me to have tea with her, or accompany her on some errand.

The last place I wanted to be was between Levi and his grandmother. And I'd barely seen him. He'd been out most days, attending meetings in Martina's stead, after ordering her to stay home and rest. Martina complained about that, too, and all I could do was sit and nod, like a good girlfriend.

This morning, after he quietly slipped away from the bedroom once again to head to a boardroom somewhere in the city, I realized that if anything happened to his grandmother—in the absence of any other male heir to the Laurent kingdom—Levi would have to take over. His father had a sister, Sandrine's mother, who had zero interest in running a business. Sandrine had no siblings. It was all up to Levi.

I had gone into the dark before, in fear that our differences would be against us, but that had been just a scratch. Levi had his own business and his own wealth, but the vastness of his family's had been beyond what Chase had managed to uncover for me. Yet, he loved me, unwaveringly. I'd be stupid to turn my back on that, wouldn't I?

Music flowed up the mezzanine of Martina's mansion. She hired a quintet to entertain the few guests who had been invited. More European royalty, I presumed.

Once Levi had caught wind of what Martina planned, he stepped in and asked her, politely, to cease with the cockamamie idea. Martina had, also politely, declined. What resulted was a smaller group of invitees for an uppity formal dinner to celebrate my boyfriend's twenty-ninth birthday.

My hands trembled as I made my way down, trying so hard not to trip on my dress, and avoiding any eye contact with the elegant people who awaited my arrival.

I swallowed whatever was stuck in my throat and held my head up high, mostly because the gold-embroidered dress made me. I wouldn't do it justice if I slumped my shoulders.

I threw in a *"bonsoir"* and *"merci"* as Martina presented me around the room, ever so pleasantly. I repeated the people's names aloud, hoping that I might remember, but they all had elegant and complicated French names, which I murdered the second they left my mouth. Some found it endearing and cute, but others regarded me like I had grown another head.

Sandrine's parents were present and stood beside their daughter. I was warmly greeted by François and sneered at by Vivienne.

Sandrine hugged me as she kissed my cheeks. "Breathe, Nica, it will be over soon," she murmured in my ear. "That is a lovely dress!"

"Thank you. Martina got it for me." I smiled at the older woman, who was more elegant than most of the women in the room, including myself.

"Bonsoir, Grand-mère." Sandrine reached forward and greeted her grandmother.

A waiter in a white tuxedo popped out of nowhere and offered us bubblies. Sandrine graciously declined. With my stomach unsettled, I, too, should have refused, but didn't. My only regret was that I wasn't alone to chug the whole flute in hopes of keeping my nervousness at bay. So I stood there and sipped, and smiled, and listened. Sandrine was kind enough to translate for me, but I had a feeling that she changed the context of her mother's opinions whenever she shared them with me *en Anglais*.

"Where's Levi?" My head must have been in the clouds. I'd been standing there for a good fifteen minutes before I even realized that he wasn't around.

"He's talking to Jacob," Sandrine replied. I waited for further explanation, but she didn't offer any. "Oh there they are." She waved at her husband, who appeared by the door looking flustered. Levi stood rigidly beside him, an unpleasant look on his face.

The two sauntered toward us, Levi not bothering to stop to greet the people who had shown up for this occasion. He faced Martina and spoke in clear, angry, rapid French. Then he turned and walked away.

Everyone around me shared a look. My heart flipped and my stomach twisted. I was an outsider.

꼬

THE LATCH CLICKED and I stepped outside into the night air. The fresh Parisian air. I inhaled the fragrance of the flowers and scent of rain that was about to come. It was good to get away for a moment. I feared that Sandrine would follow me, but I assured her that I was fine and I could find my way to a bathroom, one of sixteen in the mansion.

Instead of locking myself in a marble bathroom with gold taps, I sought out this terrace. From the windows of my room, I had a view of it. It was beautiful, and serene. I didn't know why it looked more special than the others. It just did.

I leaned forward and propped my arms over the masonry and released a heavy, cleansing sigh.

"*Bonsoir,*" a deep voice muttered behind me.

I jumped and placed a hand on my heart, which thankfully, was still attached to my veins and arteries. "Oh, crud on a cracker!"

"I didn't mean to startle you." A chuckle followed the voice. The moon and stars hid behind thick clouds, and the little lighting outside came from a couple of sconces on the walls. I could barely see him. "Would you like to have a seat?" The man who offered had a mixture of French and, if I wasn't mistaken, a British accent.

I had to remember there were affluent guests present. He could very well be one of them. And so I calmly replied, "No, thank you."

"C'mon, sugar, I don't bite." He smiled. Light or no light it was easy to see that sparkling rows of white teeth. In ghost stories, this was when the virgin girl usually got offed. Good thing I was far from virgin, and I didn't believe in ghosts. I did believe, however, in charming murderers with great teeth. I shook my head clear of the last thoughts.

I had two choices: walk back into the world where I didn't belong, or spend a few moments with this stranger who, seemingly, did not *want* to belong. My heels clicked on the paved ground as I made my way to where he was seated.

"Cigarette?" He flicked out a leather case.

I lifted a hand. "No thanks. I don't smoke. And

neither should you. It could stain your perfect teeth."
Why the hell did I say that?

The stranger paused, tilted his head at me, and chuckled. "I'll keep that in mind." He lit one, and with the light of the ember from his cigarette, I could see his features.

Hello, panty-dropper! The Marlboro man had nothing on this guy, chiselled to perfection--a square jaw, straight, regal nose, thick, dark hair that was slicked back, and if I squinted enough, I thought I could see blue eyes rimmed with unfairly thick lashes for a man.

"Are you going to stare at me all night?" He chuckled again.

I hoped it was dark enough for him to not see the blush that crawled up my neck and cheeks. "I'm just trying to see if met you. Inside, I mean." I knew I hadn't.

"Unlikely."

"Oh?"

He took a long drag from his smoke and released it in one line. "I wasn't invited." I looked down at his clothes: regular white shirt under a leather bomber jacket, and jeans. *So* not invited.

"Oh! What are you doing here, then?" He seemed harmless, fingers crossed. And friendly.

"I live here." Another long drag. Then he pushed a hand through his hair.

Was he one of the servants? A chauffeur maybe? No. A gardener? Highly unlikely. Not with his looks. Although this was Paris after all. Maybe gardeners in Paris all looked like him. Maybe I could hire him to water my lawn. I rolled my eyes at my wayward thoughts. Martina's mansion was safe and secure. Although there weren't any guards watching the grounds, alarms were set every night.

"How have I never seen you before? I've been here for three days." I took my shoes off under the long hem of my dress.

"Pardon me. I shall rephrase. I used to live here." His voice was low and rich and husky, marred by years of smoking.

"Who are you?"

He cleared his throat, switched his cigarette from one hand to the other, and stuck his right hand out. "I am Alexandre." He might as well have beaten his chest when he introduced himself.

I shook his proffered hand. "Pleasure to meet you, Alexandre." Finally, a name I could remember. Not that I would forget that face. "I'm Veronica."

"Ah, Veronica, what a lovely name. She who brings victory." It didn't slip my mind that he still held my hand.

"That's what my name means." *You charming piece of handsome pie*. Maybe that was what his name meant.

"You're American." He didn't ask a question so I kept my mouth shut. My palm in his was starting to sweat. "You're a friend of Martina's then. What brings you to Paris, Veronica?" The way he said my name made it sound salacious, rolling his 'r' and ending with 'ahhhh'.

"My boyfriend brought me here. Levi...Olivier." Alexandre's grip tightened. I knew I should have run.

He leaned forward, and pulled on my hand, which made me tilt closer to him. "Did you say he's your boyfriend?" His voice did not waver. I gulped and nodded. Then he moved back, released my hand, and laughed. No, guffawed.

Alexandre. Charming. Handsome. Psychotic. Chase would have a field day with this one.

I licked my lips, and propped a hand on my hip. "So you know each other?" I combed through my mind if Levi had ever mentioned his name before.

Alexandre made me wait for his answer, taking one last drag from his cancer stick. "You can say that."

"Good. How--"

"Veronica!" Levi sounded panicked.

I glanced at the door from where I came through. "I better go back in. Aren't you coming in too? I don't think it would matter if you weren't invited if you used to live here." I wasn't really sure, but neither was I too serious.

"Veronica?" Levi called again.

"Shit. I better go." I tried to slip my shoes back on, lifting the hem of my dress just as Levi walked out the door.

"Veronica." He sounded very worried.

"Yes, hi. Hold on. I'm putting on my shoes." Alexandre bent down and lifted one naked foot and slipped my skyscraper heel back on. Levi stalked toward me, his breathing ragged. Why was he so worked up?

"I've been looking for--" Levi paused mid-step when

he saw that I wasn't alone. My eyes had adjusted enough in the dark to see him squint his eyes. "Alexandre." Levi's voice was like a warning.

I steadied myself as my new acquaintance straightened on the bench. I looked between Levi and Alexandre. A smirk widened on Alexandre's face, as he tilted his head up and said, "Hello, little brother."

LA GOUTTE D'EAU QUI FAIT
DÉBORDER LE VASE

LEVI

*H*ow did one define a relationship? Was it by genetics shared by two individuals? Was it by experience that people had gone through? Was it by love of one and sacrifice of the other? Did relationships grow? Did they bloom, if nurtured and cared for? Did they die?

Alexandre leaned against the back of a bench. In the sparse light, I could see his grin. And in that shadow, I could feel his hatred rolling off his skin and threatening to strike me. He reached for Veronica's hand.

"I've been chatting with your girlfriend, the lovely Veronica." He lifted her hand to his lips.

I knew the game he wanted to play. But not here, not now, and never with Veronica.

She pulled her hand away, but Alexandre didn't bat an eye. He sat languorously and chuckled. "Feisty. You know how to pick them, *mon frère*," he mocked me. Every single cell in my body wanted me to wrap my hands around his neck, but I kept them fisted at my sides. It wouldn't bode well for me to go mental on him in front of her.

Veronica stood before me. "You have a brother?" The night had just gotten longer.

My eyes flitted to her. I splayed out a hand and offered it to her. "Let's go inside. We'll talk in there."

Veronica squared her shoulders, ignored my hand, and stomped past me. "You bet your ass we're going to talk." She was angry, but from the tremor in her voice I knew she was also hurt.

I sent Alexandre as much anger as I could without saying a word before chasing after Veronica.

"How could you not have told me about him?" Veronica whipped around as soon as we stepped inside. Her voice was gritty and raw. Her shoulders shook.

"Veronica, darling, I was going to..." I reached for her, but she stepped back, face determined, demanding an explanation.

"We have a sister too." It was futile to hope that Alexandre would have stayed put. Veronica shot him a surprised look, and seethed at me. "Half-sister, but a sister nonetheless."

"*Ta gueule!*" I spat at Alex, who had chosen to lean against the threshold, lighting a cigarette as he threatened, without a word, to spill everything. "Be quiet."

"Levi?" Veronica crossed her arms over her chest. "A brother and a sister? Is your dad really dead?" She pressed her lips together. But I could see she regretted asking the question.

She was teetering on the edge—either jump in with both feet with me or run and be rid of me forever.

I stepped forward again, and this time, she didn't back away. I steadied my breathing. "Sweetheart, I will explain everything later. Let's go back to the party. Have some dinner, and we'll talk. I promise." She hesitated, and I couldn't blame her.

I wrapped her in my arms and kissed her temple. I would be lost without this woman. Without her, I'd still be just like my brother, living on hate, regret, and loneliness.

Alex had decided to follow us in. I could ignore him. There were enough people around. And he had more questions to answer than I did.

❦

MY BROTHER CHOSE a chair as we seated ourselves around the dining table, far enough away that I wouldn't be tempted to stab him with a shrimp fork. The surprise of his sudden presence had quieted down, and those who were comfortable speaking with Alex did so. Veronica remained a silent observer beside me.

"You could have told me," I heard Veronica say to Sandrine. "What's the big deal anyway?"

Sandrine sent her a look of apology, and begged with her eyes for me to help her out. "E's not a secret."

"Seems like he is. Levi never told me."

Jake joined in, "He has his reasons, Nica." Jake was one of the few who didn't pay my brother any attention. Jake also knew the score.

"And a sister?" This question was directed to me.

I leaned over to reply to Veronica's question. I had promised to tell her everything. "I've never met her. Last I heard she was living in New York City."

"How could you not..."

"I promise I'll tell you everything. Please, trust me." I lowered my voice as I continued, "Now isn't the time, not with all these people."

Her lips pulled into a grim line. "I do trust you. It seems you don't trust me."

I sucked in a breath. How could she think that? Was this how trust was measured? By how many secrets were told? By how many painful memories were spilled?

"It's much more complicated than that."

"Than trust?"

We were interrupted by servers placing a gold-trimmed bowl of *soupe de poisson à la rouille* in front of us. Veronica straightened on her seat, slightly angling her body away from me. I paid attention to the food in front of me, but never bothered to lift the spoon to my mouth.

A shout pierced the hushed silence of the somber dinner. I glared at my brother.

Ladies and gentlemen: my mother. Let the trumpets sound. Let the rabid dogs free.

Lucinde Marrione Laurent entered the dining room. With an air of arrogance and displeasure, she pointed at each and every one of our guests, and spewed vitriol at Martina.

"You should leave," I said to her in my adopted language. It angered her even more.

She narrowed her blue eyes at me, clearing the distance between us with long, sure strides. Lucinde pulled her finger back before she opened her mouth. I stepped in front of Veronica to protect her.

"Leave, Mother."

My mother broke her gaze from Veronica, but my relief was short-lived, because she chose to open her mouth instead. "And miss my son's birthday? What kind of mother would I be?" Her eyes shone with malice. She waved a gloved hand to her chest, where surely her heart had withered and died. She had an audience, and she glorified in it.

"One who has never remembered her son's birthday," I replied. I felt Veronica's agitation behind me. But she reached for my hand as she stood.

My mother laughed. Loud, arid, and pernicious. She placed her hand over her empty chest again. "My darling, Olivier, you intend to hurt my feelings? In front of your guests? And...this curious creature?"

I heard Veronica scoff, ready to advance. I leaned my head to the side, trying to catch her attention, to warn her to keep steady. This wasn't her battle to fight. Veronica paused but she stayed rigid.

Ever the epitome of poise and grace, Martina offered, "Perhaps we can talk in the library, Lucinde."

"Why shouldn't I stay here? We are talking now!" Someone else caught her attention. "Why is he allowed to stay?"

"*Maman!*" I warned.

"*Lucinde, s'il vous plâit,*" Martina tried again, her voice rising.

"Shouldn't he leave? Aren't you afraid that Alexandre will steal her, like you stole his fiancée?"

In that moment, everything happened. Martina reached my mother, but she was still weak from the stroke and it showed. Jake and François moved forward to help Martina, and had her sit on a chair. My mother laughed her way out of the dining room, leaving the guests uncomfortable and concerned.

Sandrine called out a name, "Veronique!"

Veronica ran the other way. Her hand had slipped from my grasp as soon as Lucinde said those last words.

Alexandre caught my eyes. And I froze, my head hanging low, my hand reaching out for the space that Veronica had stood in.

How did one define relationships? A relationship between a mother and her sons? A relationship between two brothers? A relationship between a man and the only woman he loved?

I didn't know the answer.

COUPE DE FOUDRE

She didn't leave me. I'd deserted her.

By omitting some of the most important factors of my life, I had lied to her. Even though I knew she only deserved the truth. I had been half-honest, and a full liar. It was no wonder she wanted to get away from me.

However, I wasn't one to quit; I loved her.

She couldn't have gone far, especially not in the pouring rain. Unless she had been lucky enough to have a cab pass by as soon as she went through the gates, traveling on foot would have been her only choice. But Veronica was always innovative. She could be halfway to the airport now.

My chest tightened at that possibility. I needed to find her sooner. She had only managed to bring a small clutch to dinner, but Veronica was an expert in being prepared. She might carry her passport around at all times. If that were the case, and she'd left for San Francisco, my chances of reconciliation would dwindle.

I took the Aston Martin and drove around the block a few times. Then I went into the heart of the city. As ridiculous as it sounded, I felt that my heart had a compass in it, and it would lead me back to her. Nevertheless, every ten minutes, I called Jake and asked if she'd turned up, and each time he told me that she hadn't.

If I were Veronica, where would I go? The Louvre? It would be closed, and the rain would deter her from walking the grounds. God, I hoped she wasn't stuck somewhere, drenched in the rain.

At hour two, I turned down a narrow, slanted road, which felt familiar, but I couldn't quite figure out why. I parked along the side, ready to give Jake another ring when I saw the sign. A bar: *En Vérité*. What an odd name for such an establishment.

I stepped out of the car while connecting with Jake, and stood in front of the bar under the eaves.

"Anything?"

"No, man. Why don't you head back? She'll come here eventually. Where else would she go?" Exhaustion was present in Jake's voice.

"She has her purse with her. I don't think she'll go back there. Listen, why don't you and Sandrine go and rest? Martina will let me know if Veronica returns."

Jake sighed. "Yeah, I don't think she'll want to go until she knows Nica is safe. Martina is worried, too. Just keep us posted."

I pocketed my phone. The door to the bar opened

and a few lads scuffled out. The rain would not let up. I needed a think, and a drink, and a splash of reality. I'd made yet another fumble. A fumble? More like a catastrophe.

I stepped inside. The bar was somewhere Chase would feel welcome: dark, dingy, and inherently male. I nodded at the bartender, taking over a free stool in front of him.

"Scotch. Neat."

He nodded, and I watched him pour a small amount of golden brown liquid into a glass. He placed it in front of me and I drank it all in one gulp. The liquid burned down my throat and the warmth settled in my chest.

I signaled for another.

"*Americain?*" The bartender's voice was hoarse, probably from years of smoking.

I stared at him. I seemed to have forgotten where I was. Had I been too exhausted to act or talk like a Frenchman? What the hell? Might as well go along with it, though he would most likely charge me double for being a tourist. I nodded.

"What bring you to Paris?" he asked in a thick French accent.

I smiled over the tip of the glass, replying with, "Love," before taking another swig of the scotch.

The bartender grinned at me. "It is your lucky night, heh." He leaned forward and talked in a low, hushed voice. "An *Americaine* girl just walk in. She looks for love too. Very pretty." He smacked his fingers on his lips, and then nodded his head to the other side of the bar, past the patrons.

I lifted my head. At the corner, hunched over a similar drink to mine, was none other than the love of my life.

Perhaps my heart compass wasn't broken after all.

My pulse hitched at the sight of her, and in that moment, the world had gotten smaller, seemingly existing for only the two of us.

I returned my gaze to the bartender. I could kiss the man. I took out some notes out of my jacket pocket, and slapped it on the counter.

"Keep the change, Cupid."

He tipped his imaginary hat to me. *"Merci. Tremper le biscuit."* He made a lewd gesture with his hands. I could have done without that last bit. I sauntered over to where Veronica sat.

I trained my eyes at her, willing for hers to meet mine as soon as I turned that corner, but her focus was only on her drink. Her mouth parted, and from where I stood, I could almost hear her sigh. I could almost feel the warmth of her breath. I wanted to rush over to her, wrap her in my arms and never let go.

"Veronica…" I wanted her to hear sincerity, feel my honesty, and believe in my undying love.

All she did was look past me. Would she ever forgive me?

She stood slowly, brushed a tendril of hair from her forehead, and walked away, abandoning her drink and me. I reached for her, but she quickened her steps, and my fingers only grasped the empty air.

Bar patrons huddled between us, greeting each other and blocking me from running after her. I pushed through and took one last glance at the bartender. He nodded at me, as though telling me to go after the girl. I intended to.

The rain pelted the uneven streets when I stepped out, harder than it had earlier. I could see Veronica make her way toward the corner of the street.

I was too stubborn to let that happen. I went after her, slipping as I turned the corner. The street was busy with people-- friends, lovers, workers, tourists. Some huddled underneath their coats, and others held umbrellas. I held onto hope.

From where I stood, I saw a vision. A woman with long dark hair, glistening like the rain illuminated by the night lights. I took a couple of long strides to get nearer her, dodging everyone else. When she was within reach. I called her name.

She stopped and turned.

I loved this woman. But would she accept me as the broken man that I was?

"Please..."

Veronica took a step back. "Your brother's fiancée, Levi?"

"Let me explain." My heart thudded.

The rain pelted us, people passed us by, murmuring and gawking.

"My mother, she...she wanted to hurt us. She would do anything to hurt me."

"I don't care about your mother! I cared that you've kept me in the dark this whole time. A brother?" She stared up at the dark skies. "Not once did you mention a brother, and now I know why!"

"It wasn't like that. Just come with me, let's go back to Martina's and I'll explain everything."

She bit her lip and looked down at her own hands, wrinkled from the rain. One hand clutched her small handbag. Veronica trembled. Her hair was soaked, her dress was ruined, and the rain washed the luminescence off her skin and replaced it with cold, glistening defiance.

I took off my coat and wrapped it around her.

She didn't push me away.

"My car is right around the corner. Let me take you back, get you all dried up, and we can talk properly."

"No.... There." She pointed at a lit sign beside us. Her teeth chattered. With my arm around her, I could feel her body shivering. It could be from anger or the cold.

I guided her toward the entrance, let her lean against me. We walked to the man standing at the desk, watching us drip rainwater on his shiny floor. I reached for my cards, inside my jacket draped over Veronica. I sighed as my hand felt the strong thud of her heartbeat and the heat of her skin.

"*Avez-vous une chambre disponsible?*" I asked, pushing a black card toward the man as I inquired for an available room.

He picked up the credit card. "*Oui, Monsieur.*" He typed on a keyboard.

"I want the same room. Seventh floor. 712," Veronica told him, her voice steady. The man paused and looked my way. I nodded.

"*Oui, mademoiselle*. It is available for the night. Just for one night?" The man asked.

"*S'il vous plait*. Please," I replied.

He returned to his monitor. I kept a hold on Veronica as I answered each one of his questions. My own teeth had started to chatter as well. The adrenaline rush was running off. I had to fight it from wearing me down. I needed the energy to face the dark past that I was about to reveal.

WE STOOD an arm's length apart inside the elevator. Veronica stepped out first, turned the corner, and stood waiting for me to slide the key in and unlock the door.

The light from the city danced with the shadows of the room. I wasn't quite sure, but Veronica would know if it was the same as the last time we'd been here. This was the very room where I had poured my heart out.

Veronica kept walking to the middle of the room, pausing beside the bed. She took off the coat and hung it over the footboard and placed her purse on the mattress. I turned the other way, toward the bathroom, and brought back two towels. I returned and stood before her to wrap a dry towel over her soaked skin and hair. My hands shook and I breathed out jagged air as I patted her skin dry.

Yet Veronica said nothing. She refused to glance my way. I could feel the fight within her. I knelt in front of her, and helped her out of her shoes. Her hand, light and steady, was on my shoulder for support. Once I finished with the task I'd taken, I stayed on my knees, looked up to her, and breathed. "Forgive me."

It didn't matter what my mother said or how she'd said it. I kept it a secret from Veronica. I would understand if she told me that she'd never want to see me again. It would be painful but I would understand. I was holding onto the small thread of hope I had left that she would at least hear me out to the very end when I opened up wounds.

The loss of love—her love, Veronica's—was almost tangible and it consumed me. A mélange of pain and agony awaited. And that feeling of emptiness without her prickled behind my closed lids.

"My sweet Veronica, my love..."

Her hand rested on my shoulder then stroked up my neck and the side of my face. "Levi." I waited to hear more. But what came out soon after were heavy sighs. Veronica unwrapped my arms from her, and sat on the bed. "Come sit with me," she said in a quiet, tremulous voice.

She looked out into the night. "I didn't know where to go when I left. All I remembered was the address of this hotel. I knew it by heart. But I couldn't go in. It didn't feel right. So I walked around and ended up at the bar. *Vérité*. It means truth, right? I just wanted the truth." My hands itched to touch her, my lips ached to kiss her, but I waited for her to continue. "Tell me about your brother and his fiancée."

I wished she would glance my way, offer me some promise that no matter what I was about to tell her, no matter what I'd say, she would still love me. She wanted the truth. I ached for a promise that she would remain by my side to see this through. My heart thumped angrily in my chest. My hands trembled as I faced her, and all my uncertainties. Would she still love me even after I removed the mask and showed her the ugly truth? After knowing how fractured a man I was?

With my heart thick in my throat, I stared her in the eyes and held her hands.

Then I opened my heart and let it bleed.

Á L'OMBRÉ DE L'AMOUR

"*I*t has been ten years."

I removed my soaked shirt and grabbed the robes from the closet. I draped one over Veronica and used the other. The chill that clung to me wasn't from the rain. "Alex was engaged for a year before they set a date. Their wedding was set for the same time I was to leave France for the U.S."

"What was her name?" Veronica's voice was flat.

"Simone." I hadn't uttered the name in a decade. "She was a model, from an affluent family. It was an arranged marriage, or something of the sort, at first. Something like Sandrine's mother tried to do with her and Gaspard. After several months, Alex and Simone learned to respect and love each other."

"How old was she? And Alex?"

"They were both twenty-one. Young, too young. Martina thought so too, but my father wouldn't listen.

Simone's father was an influential man. A politician. My father had big plans for Alex."

Veronica slightly angled her head towards me. "And you?"

'Insignificant' was the word that came to mind. "I was just a kid who partied too much and cared too little."

I waited for her to ask another question, but she just stared out the windows, and so I continued, "Alex and I were close. He looked after me a lot, especially when we were much younger. Kept me out of too much trouble until I started finding it on my own. He didn't like the idea of me leaving, but it wasn't up to either of us. My father had decided, and so it would be. Alex was being groomed to take over the family business. It didn't matter if I failed any of my classes, or even if I continued my education. He was it. The golden son."

"Were you jealous? Wanting what your brother had?"

It took a minute before I could formulate the proper words. "Perhaps. A little. My parents didn't agree on much, but they were both so proud of him, and his accomplishments. It took me a while to realize I wanted that too. Alex hated it though. He once confessed to me that he wanted to be a nomad, an artist who travelled the world. I suppose he did get his wish."

"What...What do you mean?"

I brushed my hair back, still dripping rainwater on my shoulders, leaned forward, and propped my head on my hands. "When he left Paris, he travelled around the world as a photographer."

"Hmmm. Where do you and Simone fit in the picture?" Her voice faltered as she said the name.

"Simone and I became close too. I dated a lot of her friends. We partied quite a bit together. Alex didn't like it much, but it was another way for him to look after me. He entrusted me with Simone, and vice versa."

The tip of Veronica's chin tilted up as she inhaled deeply. "And that was when the betrayal happened?" she breathed out.

"There was no betrayal. Not on my part." Veronica finally looked my way. I straightened, letting her see the truth in my eyes. "Simone and I never happened. She came to me one night, panicked. She was delirious. I thought she was high, but she wasn't. She kept saying that Alex would cast her aside if he found out the truth. I tried to clarify, but she kept repeating herself, over and over that Alex would hate her. He wouldn't want to marry her. She was tainted. Then Alex came."

I buried my face in my hands. "I had been at a party earlier, and before Simone came to me, a girl had just left my apartment. Alex busted in. It just so happened that Simone and I were in my bedroom. I had followed her in there when she came to me, frantic. Alex saw the bed, saw me practically naked, and Simone..." I shook my head at the memory of that night. "All she said was that I was just a kid. That he should take it easy on me. Alex had been my protector. My brother and I had never fought, but that night he beat me 'til I could barely breathe."

Veronica gasped at my revelations. "Why didn't you defend yourself? Why didn't you tell him the truth?"

Those were the same questions I had asked myself for years. "I have never been good at opening up. All Alex saw was the person who took the only good thing he had in his life."

I struggled to breathe as the memories of that painful night rose to the surface. I thought I had forgotten the pain of losing my brother. I thought finding Veronica had cured me of it. "Simone called for an ambulance when Alex left. A week later...Alex left for good." Heaviness stayed on my chest. I struggled to breathe. "I found out that Simone was pregnant when she came to see me, but she lost the baby soon after. I think she lost all hope after that. Three months later, Simone died of an accidental overdose." I felt the prickles behind my eyes, but I refused to let them flow. I had shed enough tears for Simone and Alex.

I could feel the tremor from Veronica's body even as I kept space between us.

"Simone had cheated on my brother and it resulted in a pregnancy. When she confessed to Alex, she inferred it was with someone close to him. He was livid, and then she came to me, afraid." I released a sigh that was choking me. "I wondered for years why she got me involved. Alex wouldn't have thought that I would...but he did, because I was the kind of person who would do such a thing. Not to him though. Never to my brother. I loved him. He and Martina were all I had. Simone too, in some ways." I turned my head and held Veronica's gaze. "You must believe me, Veronica, I never touched her."

"If it wasn't with you, who was—"

145

"It was my father." The truth hurt. It was a stab to my heart. The truth would set me free, but it could also destroy me, and what I had with Veronica. "My mother knew, and she did nothing." I struggled to get the words out, but Veronica had to know everything. "She let us all ruin ourselves. I don't know when she found out about Simone and my father, and all she said was that it didn't matter if we knew. We'd end up like him—a cheater, incapable of loving one woman. I guess now you can see why I'm so messed up when it comes to...love and relationships. Apart from my grandparents, no one in my family had ever had an honest marriage, or a happy one."

Our breath was all I could hear for a while until she asked, "How about Sandrine's parents?"

I shook my head. "François is Vivienne's third husband. They have an ironclad pre-nup, and they had Sandrine. My cousin was enough to keep her parents together, difficult as it may be for François. But he stayed for his daughter."

There was a slight shift on the mattress, yet Veronica continued to avoid contact with me. "Why is your mother so...angry at you if she knew you had nothing to do with it?"

I expelled a dry chuckle, humorless, weak. "Lucinde is angry at the world." I rubbed my temples, trying to expel that pain that clamped around my head. "Once upon a time, she was in love with my father, and thought he would offer her the moon. It wasn't long after they got married that he started cheating on her.

146

This went on for years. She kept holding on to hope though. When she had Alex, she thought my father would stop. He did for a while, but it didn't last. By the time I came into the picture, the love and hope had run out. Her heart hardened."

"But you always had Alex. You said it yourself, he cared for you."

"Yes." I nodded. "Until he didn't want me as his brother anymore." The burden of my own words weighed heavily on my shoulders. I hung my head low, ashamed of the life I had lived, of the chaos that I'd let rule it. "I just never thought true love existed for me...until I met you."

Veronica stayed quiet for a moment and took a long, cleansing breath. Would she take me back now that she knew all the skeletons I'd hidden away? Would she see me as a tainted man with no hope of a future with the likes of her?

"Levi," she began. I slowly lifted my head and waited. She reached for my hand.

My heart banged against my chest. Was this a sign that she trusted me again? That she forgave my lacking? With my free hand, I pushed her hair aside and ran my hand up the column of her neck. I pulled her close to me and inhaled her unique scent, made sweeter by the rain.

"Stop, please," Veronica asked quietly. I lowered my hand, but kept the other one gripped in hers, holding onto it like it was my lifeline. "I'm going to need some time to think. I'm sorry, but it's a lot to take in."

I had questions to ask. I had words to say, but the way her heart-shaped mouth formed into a set line kept me silent. I lifted her hand to my lips and placed a kiss of promise.

§

THE RAIN HAD STOPPED before I stepped outside. I struggled not to return to Veronica, but how would she react to me if I did? What I had given her was a window to a past that had influenced me as a man. But it was one part of my entire being. Being with her had shown me a different kind of man I could be, that I wanted to be, for her and for us.

The concierge at the desk had given me a curious look when I'd faced him again, requesting that I be notified if Veronica decided to leave the hotel. I'd ordered him to give her whatever she requested, for however long she wanted to stay there.

I shrugged my jacket on as I made my way to the car and felt the vibrating in my pocket. I pulled out my phone.

"Levi," Jake said in a tired voice.

"Yeah."

"Did you find her?"

"I did."

He breathed out a relieved sigh. "Good. You should come back. Martina fainted again. We're monitoring her now."

I paused mid-step as I heard the news. "When?"

"A half hour ago. We tried to call you. She came to,

and her heart rate is steady now. We've given her some heavy medication. She's asking for you."

"I'll be there." I rang off, and looked back to the hotel. In there was where my heart lay, but duty called me home.

LEUR CŒUR S'EMBRASSENT

*S*ilence greeted me as I entered the mansion. All the guests had gone, except for Sandrine and Jake. My feet, heavy and soaked with the past as much as rainwater, dragged as I climbed the stairs. As I faced my Onna's bedroom door, I fought to steady my breathing.

I expected a lot more life in the bedroom but what I came into was a barely lit room and the sound of a heart monitor. The beeping meant that Martina kept on fighting.

She was on her back, with a thick duvet over her. She looked peaceful, such a contrast to my chaotic state. I sat on the edge of her bed, reached over, and tucked a tendril of hair behind her ear.

"She's been given a mild sedative." A voice shot out of the darker side of the room.

I cocked my head at the source, but I didn't fully turn. Rage built within me. "Shouldn't you be halfway around the world by now? You've caused enough problems to last a lifetime." I let the vitriol spew out of my veins.

"I didn't come here to cause..."

"Then why? Why did you come back?"

"Because it was time." Alex stepped into the light, walking around the large canopy bed. He appeared as exhausted as I was, with dark circles around his eyes, a furrow line on his forehead and a mouth forced into a frown. "Where's Veronica?"

I was on my feet in an instant, fists ready at my sides. "Don't," I warned.

"You need to calm down." He used the same tone that he had when I was a teenager.

I laughed drily. "You think you have the right to say that to me?"

He hung his head, and worked a hand over his chin. "It's been too long. Must we bring up the past?"

"I wouldn't have to, if you hadn't shown up!" I yelled again, pushing a hand on his chest, but he stayed where he stood.

Alex pointed a steady finger at me. "I asked you to keep your voice down," he warned.

The monitor beeped loudly. I glanced at Martina, still asleep. She produced a light groan, but didn't open her eyes. I knew she could hear us. Even in her sleep state, I'd managed to stress her out.

"You want to talk? Come outside."

I didn't wait for Alex. I grabbed the handle of the door and flung it open. As soon as he stepped out, I shuffled forward and pushed him against the paneled wall, my forearm heavy on his neck.

"You ruined the best thing that has happened in my life!" I accused him.

Alex did not struggle. I had grown far from the young kid he had beaten up ten years ago. I had the strength to match his, and the hatred that fuelled it.

"Levi!" Jake appeared at my side, and held my arm, which pushed against Alex's trachea. "Let go."

I clenched my jaw and gritted my teeth, exhaling a loud breath as I released Alex. He doubled over, trying to breathe. Sandrine stood with her hands on her round stomach and worry in her eyes.

"I'm sorry." His words came out in a huff. "I'm sorry, Levi," Alex said again. He straightened, his hands splayed in front of him. "I lost my temper with the wrong person."

To hear those words... I had been ready to accept that our relationship would never be repaired. The Laurent brothers did not patch things up. We sailed on through, ignoring the musts and the shoulds, living in the agony of our disastrous past.

I'd thought of this moment for so long, however, that at some point in my life, I'd given up on it. And now that it was here, I didn't know what to do.

Sandrine reached out for Jake and silently asked him to let us be. They both placed their hands on my back, a reminder that they'd be there for me, no matter what.

"How much do you know?" Alex asked me.

"All of it."

He leaned against the railing to my side, his hands folded over his chest.

"And you?" I asked him.

"All of it."

"How?"

"How do you think?" Alex stared straight on.

I turned to glance at Martina's bedroom door. Had Martina shared everything with him? But why would she? And why didn't she tell me?

"She came to me when I was in Morocco, and asked me to come home. Told me that your scars have healed. I told her that I couldn't. That the scars I left behind were deeper than the eyes could see."

I scoffed. "Don't go melodramatic at my expense."

"I'm not, brother. I knew what I did was wrong. And I knew that it would take a while before you could forgive me, if you ever will."

"And you think I'm ready to forgive you now?" I spat angrily at him.

Alex copied my stance, except as my hands were fisted at my sides, his was stretched out. "Yes."

"What makes you think that?"

"Because you have found love. And I hoped that you'd understand why I reacted the way I did."

"Don't make it an excuse!"

"It's not. But you do understand, don't you?"

"What if I don't?"

He hung his head. "Then you can never forgive me."

"I almost died. I had six fractured ribs. One nearly punctured my lung. I spent months in rehab, underwent two surgeries."

"And they've healed. Those scars have been gone for years. But the others..." His eyes were direct, burrowing through to see my soul.

"I think you should leave."

"I'm not going anywhere," Alex said firmly.

"I'll have you arrested for trespassing." I made my way towards the stairs, leaving him standing by the rails.

"Trespassing in my own home?"

I was incredulous. "This isn't your home!"

"But it is." Alex angled his head toward Martina's room.

My thoughts jumbled; my head shook. I rubbed my temples. "She wouldn't do that."

"She has. It's done. The ink dried months ago."

No.

"She came to me in the spring. When you asked for the ring."

I didn't know what Alex was playing at. My legs weakened underneath me, and I braced myself against the stairway rails. My mind went back to Veronica, how she had seemed so utterly destroyed by my omission of the truth. This, what I felt now deep within shrouding over my heart, this was what she had felt. I surrendered to the weakness and sat on a step.

Alex joined me, and I was filled with the distinct memories of the times we had done this when we were young. Two brothers huddled at the top of the stairs, waiting for a miracle.

"She didn't want to tell you until you were ready," he said in *sotto voce*.

"The stroke..." I pushed my fingers through my hair as I tried to make sense of everything.

"I found her." The words had me staring at my brother's eyes, bluer than mine, filled with despair. "Martina said that you'd brought Veronica to your vineyard to propose to her. She'd been so sure that you'd be calling with the good news. And she wanted me here to listen 'to the adoration of a man in love'."

I could picture and hear Martina say those words. "It didn't happen. I had to fly here."

"I gathered that. When I came back, I wasn't sure how I'd be received. Martina had assured me that all would be forgotten. Mother didn't know I was around, not until tonight. Martina and I were finalizing some paperwork—all while we waited for was the news of your engagement."

"Why would she wait for that?"

"When Martina came to me with the news of Veronica, she was ecstatic. You'd finally found love, she said. With an American girl. And from that moment on, she knew you wouldn't come back. I was skeptical, of course. You could guess why. But when she told me about the ring, I began to wonder if she was right after all. And I had to see it for myself. We were setting up to see you in California, visit the vineyard you're so proud of, and meet the woman who has captured your heart."

"She asked me to leave tonight." The words were out before I could stop them.

"And you left her?"

"Was else could I do?" Frustrated with myself, I smashed my head into my hands.

"You could have stayed, fought for that love."

"The way you did?"

Alex released a heavy sigh before he answered, "That wasn't love. It was pride and hurt, pain and sorrow. If Simone had loved me, truly loved me, she wouldn't have succumbed to another man's charms and empty promises."

"Have you forgiven him? Or Simone?"

My brother stayed quiet, looking straight on past the grand chandelier. He couldn't answer me, because he didn't know. I knew he didn't know. To be in that much desperation and darkness for so long—I could only imagine.

"Where are you going?" Alex asked as I stood.

"To get her back," I stated, plain and simple. We had quite a bit more work in our relationship, but I had my priorities.

"Honestly, Levi, I don't think you've ever lost her." He nodded his head once toward the front of the house, like he saw something I'd missed. And a few moments later, a knock on the door echoed in the hallway.

My feet couldn't move fast enough down the stairs. I gripped the handle, breathed in, and opened the door.

LE CŒUR DU BONHEUR

"*V*eronica."

Her lips trembled as she locked eyes with me. A gush of wind whipped the hair behind her when she stepped inside. "I came as soon possible. I didn't check my phone until... how is she?"

"How did you get here?"

"Sandrine sent a car. How is she, Levi? How's Martina?"

"She's resting now. Jake said she'll be fine. You returned for her?"

She captured her bottom lip between her mouth, staring at the floor. "I didn't want you to be alone. I was worried."

I would fight the world for this woman, but it seemed she'd fight for me too. I cupped her chin in my hands and slowly lifted her head, urging her to see me, a man broken, a man splintered, who loved her with every fiber of his soul. Agony, fear, loneliness and desperation didn't hold a candle to what I felt for her.

It was love, pure and simple.

Inhaling her scent, I inched forward, ghosting my lips over hers, feeling the tremor coursing through her body. When I exhaled, she breathed it in. And I knew then that she was my life, and I was hers.

"Levi, I'm so sorry," she uttered before I pressed my lips on hers, tasting her sweetness once again. It wasn't a long kiss, but it was full of passion and fervency, creating a sizzle through me. I leaned my forehead against hers, continuing to live in the moment. Her eyes were closed. Her hands riffled through my hair and massaged the nape of my neck. Her heartbeat thrummed against mine, a symphony between us.

I kissed her again, and nibbled at her lip, repeating her name over and over, in whispers, through trembles, "Veronica, my Veronica, there's nothing you should apologize for. I was the one who was wrong. I shouldn't have left."

"I shouldn't have let you go. I've been so stupid. So foolish." Her hands reached down and held onto mine. I brought them to my lips, afraid to let them go.

"You're here now. We're here together. That's all that matters."

We stood there for a while, leaning against each other for strength and support.

"I'd like to see her."

"Of course." With my lips, I smoothed the worry lines on her forehead. I wrapped my arms around her, squeezing her against me, before I led her up the stairs.

Alex was nowhere to be found, though Jake and Sandrine stood at the end of the hall. Veronica waved at them, and they waved back before retreating to their room.

We entered Martina's bedroom as quietly as we could. She hadn't changed position. The machine kept its rhythm. My phone buzzed in my pocket, but I ignored it. I was aware that it could very well be the concierge from the hotel, fulfilling his promise.

"Her blood pressure spiked, and she fainted, but it wasn't another stroke." I spoke in a calm manner. There was no need to scare Veronica.

"That's good to know. Jake said all she needed was a good night's sleep?" I nodded, even though Veronica kept staring at Martina.

"You'll see her in the morning. She'd be glad to see you're back...You are back, aren't you, my darling?"

She nodded. "Let's let her rest." Veronica approached Martina's bed and leaned over to kiss her forehead. "See you in the morning, Onna."

"Where'd you learn that word?"

"She asked me to call her that. I've been too shy to say it until now." Simple words, yet they spoke volumes.

Veronica reached out for my hand, led us out of the room and towards the east wing of the mansion, where our bedroom awaited.

❧

THE DOOR CLICKED CLOSED, and we were engulfed in

darkness. My pulse thudded in my ears. My hands shook.

When the light switched on, Veronica stood by the bed, picking up a small brown box. She placed a hand over her parted lips.

"What is it?" I sauntered to her. She lifted the box and presented it to me, urging me silently to open it.

"Open it," she encouraged.

I ripped the indistinct wrapping off, and pulled apart the flap of the small box. Inside it was a much more elegantly wrapped box with silver paper and a red bow. The tag read, "With love, Veronica". I glanced up at her with a mixture surprise and question in my eyes. "For me?"

SHE NODDED, and approached me, placing a hand over mine, which held the gift. I pulled out my present, a watch. A hiccup choked in my throat, as I stared at it. "Happy Birthday, my love," Veronica said before she kissed one corner of my lips.

"You got a me a present?"

"Yes. Do you like it?"

"I..." My legs felt weak. I let myself fall on the bed, sitting on the edge, with the opened box held in one hand before me. "I've never received a present before."

"What do you mean never?" Veronica was careful not to touch me, but she pinned me with the fervent look in her eyes. "Never?"

"Yeah. No one has ever given me anything for my

birthday. My parents often forgot it. It wasn't anything my brothers and I got used to."

I was certain Veronica had other questions she wanted to ask, but those were forgotten for the moment. Her eyes welled up. She lifted the box from my hand and took out the watch. "It has an inscription on the back." She turned over and let me read it.

"With you I feel whole."

She flipped the watch over and waited until I raised my arm to her. Then she clasped it on my wrist. "Those were your words the night you told me you love me. 'I am far from perfect, but with you I feel whole.'" Once she was done, she fluttered kisses on the knuckles of my hands.

Veronica tugged and I stood. With as much tenderness as I could muster, I whispered a hand over her face, pushing tendrils of her hair behind her ears.

The night sky had cleared and the bright moonlight shone into the room. It didn't quite reach Veronica but to me she was luminescent. Her chest raised and lowered as she breathed steadily, running her fingers over my shirt. She thumbed the lapels of my jacket, pushing it off my chest and letting it drop to the floor. One by one, she worked at my buttons. I wondered if she could she how heavily my heart thudded in my chest. The warmth of her fingertips seared my skin as she drew lines and circles over my chest and all the way down past my navel.

The rest of my clothes joined the pile on the floor. I stayed standing in a state of undress, letting her take it all in-- scars, imperfections, flaws–to see what she wanted to see as she stepped back. She raised her eyes and held my gaze. And I waited.

Her dress pooled by her feet as she unzipped it and let it slide down her body. There she was, my Veronica, my goddess, with the moonlight trying to reach the silhouette of her curves.

I offered my hands for her to take and she accepted. The same hands stroked up her arms and caused a sizzle between us. I kept the watch on and its ticking was drowned out by the rapid tattoo of my heart. Unhurriedly, I invited Veronica into the bed, laying her head on the cool, silk sheets.

I basked in her sweet warmth.

As though I was starved, I kissed her. I kissed her lips, her cheeks, the coil of her ears. I kissed the tips of her fingers, the pulse on her wrists, the soft skin inside her elbows. I kissed the column of her neck, the dip of her throat, the smoothness between her breasts. All the while, my hands ghosted over the curve of the edge of her ribs down the bend of her waist and to the arc of her hips.

My Veronica. I placed my ear on her chest, and listened to the whispers of her heart. I gazed up at her eyes and swam in the pools of desire. Between my lips, I captured her cupid's bow, and inhaled the sigh of her breath. I filled her with everything I had, memorized the sensation of her around me, and embraced her body as she bowed underneath me.

We moved as one, as though we were united beyond any physicality, where her skin didn't end but continued with mine. She dug her fingers on my back as I pushed, taking her with me to where all emotions gathered. The only soundtrack we had were the symphony of our exhales, the gasps of our inhales, the mewl from her lips, and the moan from my mouth.

And when we were at the precipice, she whispered my name, "Levi". I stared into her eyes and took us both over the edge, answering her with her own, "Veronica."

I loved this woman. And I knew she loved me, scars, cuts, bruises and all. She had accepted me, cleared off the webs from my past and made way to a better future. She had cleansed me of my sorrows and delighted with me in the heat of our love. She is my goddess, my sweet, my all.

Releasing her slowly, I lay on my side. She curved towards me, fitting into the crevice of my body, crossing my legs with hers as I wrapped an arm around her. Veronica lowered her head and rested it against my chest. Her jagged breath fluttered and warmed my skin. "I love you," she whispered.

"And I love you," I said back. Our hands intertwined between our thumping hearts.

I closed my eyes and dreamt of a future with my Veronica who had shown me in many ways that I was completed. I was whole. I was loved.

VEUS TU M'APOUSER?

"**W**ill you marry me?"

I tested the words under my breath. My heart thundered in my chest. A lump had formed in my throat. As I cleared it, Veronica wriggled beside me, peacefully asleep.

Her eyes didn't flutter open, and I was relieved. It wasn't because I was not ready, but what if... I had to get a grip. The past couple of times I'd planned to do this had turned into disasters. I looked around the brightly-lit bedroom. No signs of imminent danger here. Just a perfect opportunity.

One of my arms was stuck under her, and when Veronica slept, she was an unmovable rock. I had to reach for the bedside table without waking her up. Every time I moved an inch, she snuggled closer. A bit more and I was almost there. I might have suffered a strain on my shoulder but I needed to retrieve the box from the drawer. It slammed shut, and my eyes darted back to Veronica to make sure the noise didn't wake her.

I placed the box over my chest, feeling the thrum of my heartbeat underneath it. I opened it and pulled out the ring. The diamond caught the light and glistened. A prism of colors danced around us.

꿈

AFTER THE THIRD KISS, she opened her eyes into slits. She made that cute little sound with her pursed lips-- almost a purr. Veronica wriggled her nose and smiled before she opened her eyes.

"Crap, my contacts!" She blinked furiously, lifted her hands to rub her eyes, but she stopped before she could do any damage to her corneas.

"Good morning to you too," I said with a chuckle, kissing the tip of her nose.

"Mornin', babe." Veronica pressed one side of her head to the pillows, with a Cheshire cat-like grin, her hair a dark contrast to the white sheets. She kept her eyes closed. "I should take them off now."

"Sweetheart, can you just open your eyes for a moment?" And see me presenting her with a ring...

"No, babe, hold on," she tilted her head up, squinting. "I'll be quick."

She moved to get up, which was a bad idea since I had a tray of breakfast beside her. The tray jostled, the cup of hot chai latté I had prepared for her tipped and spilled all over the bed, and onto my lap.

"Oh!" Veronica jumped off the bed, set the tray aside and began patting my hot—and not in a good way—crotch, while I hopped on one foot. "Why didn't you tell me there was hot food on the bed?"

"I was trying to surprise you." I hoped to God my bits weren't singed. In retrospect, hot latté on the bed was a terrible idea. "I thought it would be romantic."

Veronica giggled. She was on her knees now, continuing to pat my soaked trousers with her hands, which had other effects than keeping the heat off my skin. "This is not working. Just take off your pants." She didn't have to tell me twice.

Before Veronica lifted herself off the floor, she grabbed the shirt I had discarded last night. I loved it when she wore my shirt. It looked sexier on her.

As I reached for the button of my trousers, she pointed at the box in my hand. I'd picked it up to save it from the latté explosion.

"What's that?"

Her round eyes pulled me in. I opened my mouth to speak.

It wasn't how I pictured doing this. I ignored the heat spreading on my legs, and went for it.

I got down on one knee and clasped her hand into mine. I had a long preamble prepared for this exact moment, but that all went out the window when the tray tipped. And I was left only with the most important words. "Veronica, will you marry me?"

Pure and simple. It was always going to be like this.

Veronica's eyes welled up, as she pressed a hand on her lips. She nodded and whispered, "Yes."

A smile spread on my face. I picked the ring out and placed it on her... "Wrong hand," I muttered, shaking my head and laughing at myself. Veronica joined in with the laughter and offered her trembling left hand. The ring slipped onto her finger. Perfect.

"Levi, it's beautiful." Her eyes glistened like the diamond in the sunshine.

As I stood, I let my hands wander over her legs, her hips, her waist, and ended up cupped behind her neck. "*Je t'aime pour toujours*. I will always love you." They were more than words. They were a promise.

"*Je t'aime à fond*," Veronica whispered before I crushed my lips on hers.

It didn't matter how I asked her. No grand gestures were required. Not a private spot between the Redwoods, or a picnic in the vineyard. All I needed was a spot with her in it. Although I was sure she'd have a blast once I told her stories of my failed attempts.

After that long, searing kiss, Veronica sighed against my lips. "Levi..."

"Yeah?" I kept her wrapped in my arms, listening to the thrum of our heartbeats.

"When we tell people, can we say..."

"I know, skip the spilled latté and burnt crotch."

She snickered against my lips. "No, I'd like to tell them every perfect moment, down to the soaked pants, and my lack of underwear." Veronica laughed again, a sweet easy sound. "Okay, maybe not the lack of underwear part."

Why wouldn't we? This was our story to tell.

❧

WE SORTED OURSELVES OUT, ensured that my sensitive bits didn't need first aid and were still functional. I had checked in on Martina before bringing Veronica breakfast in bed, so I knew that my Onna would be waiting for the good news.

Sandrine and Jake in the gardens had joined her when Veronica and I stepped out. Kisses and embraces were exchanged, as well as the expected words of congratulations.

Alex came back, after having attended a final meeting with the family's solicitors. With Veronica beside me, I extended an olive branch, inviting my brother to visit California once he was done helping out Martina. Our grandmother was pleased with this progress, and I had to say, so was I.

Veronica's phone rang. She had sent an email to Chase and her family about our engagement, and promised a Skype call in the afternoon. I guessed someone couldn't wait any longer. I could tell by her short replies that my dear love was on the phone with her best friend. She rang off almost too quickly.

"Everything okay?" I asked, leaned in for a kiss while I wrapped her hand in mine.

"Chase."

"Hmmm." Chase was an enigma, but one thing for sure—she cared for Veronica. Whether her attitude toward me would change or not, now that Veronica and I were engaged, was anyone's guess.

Martina's butler came out with champagne and we all toasted a new beginning. I turned to my bride-to-be and felt my heart skip a beat. Only she could do that to me. Only Veronica, my sweet, my goddess, my forever after.

EPILOGUE: WHITE GOSSAMER

VERONICA

"Heave. Inhale. Cough. Heave some more. What the heck was I thinking?

Outside, past the elegant curtain swags, I could hear the clinking of glasses and the chatter of busy bees, my friends and colleagues. Fifty people made an effort to come here and witness me taking that sacred vow. But I couldn't face them. Not yet.

Heave. Breathe. Cough.

In braids and swooped into a bun, threaded with fresh flowers, my hair looked elegant, yet simple. My combination birdcage and blusher veil was propped atop a bust. It would pair so well with the vintage dress I had chosen. With Diego's help, I'd managed to keep the weight off, despite the constant eating and drinking. I'd begged Levi to stop cooking for me, but he wouldn't listen. He'd always believed food, in general, was an aphrodisiac. Who needed that when I had the love of my life?

I tiptoed around the claw foot tub and peeked out the window, behind the gossamer fabric. In two seconds flat I spotted Levi with his head thrown back as he laughed. Gerard was flailing around, recalling an incident that had happened at a previous wedding, where the white peacocks the bride had insisted on began mating during the ceremony. That night, I'd crossed any live animals, birds or otherwise, off my own wedding list. Mateo swiped his cheeks with the back of a hand, chuckling at his husband.

Levi was at ease, so relaxed in the presence of my friends. Such a difference to how I was feeling at the moment. Inhale. Heave. Heave. My heart pounded. There was a thin ringing in my ear. A headache was brewing.

How could I let this happen?

My sister, Maggie, swerved around the other guests to get to Levi. Oh, how I loved the smile he offered my sister as she leaned forward, whispering something into his ear. His smile crept into confusion, then worry. I saw Maggie point a finger at my window, well, the bathroom window. I backed away, making sure that they didn't see me, and looked at the only way out. The door had a padded bench in front of it. I'd put it there.

I walked around the tub again, where my vintage-inspired gown lay—an embroidered and beaded custom piece made especially for this occasion—and sat on the bench. My knees knocked against each other as I propped my elbows on them.

"Nica, dear, why don't you open the door? I'm sure we can talk about this. It's just nerves," my mother said through the thick, carved wood. She followed that with a couple of raps. "Nica, open up, sweetie." She had been trying for over half an hour now.

I sat straight and spread my arms. I hated being nervous. When I get out of here, I'd be stinking of anxiety and sweat. There was no way I could let that happen. I leaned my head against the door, and turned to press my ear on it.

There were a few mumbles behind the door, and then Chase's loud voice flowed through, "Hey, Nica! I get it. It's freaky. You're freaking out. I mean, one guy for the rest of your life?"

"Chase!" At least three other people yelled.

"What? I'm just telling the truth! If she doesn't want to get married today, then let her think about it some more. This vineyard isn't going anywhere. Levi's not going anywhere..."

Her voice quieted down. And I knew then that Levi was inside the room. Even through the thickness of the wooden door, I could feel his presence. It should have been enough to calm me, but instead, it caused me more panic. I looked around the bathroom to see if there was a bag I could breathe into. I was hyperventilating, and if I wasn't careful, I'd pass out. My eyes dropped to the white bag on the vanity and grabbed it.

Breathe into the bag. A piece of paper flew into my mouth. I plucked it out and saw that it was a receipt. After making sure that the bag was empty, I tried again. Breathe into the bag. Breathe out. In and out.

A quiet knock made me pause. I caught my wide, wild eyes on the mirror.

"Sweetheart, is there something you'd like to talk about?"

Levi. My chest tightened. I bet he didn't see this coming. No one had seen this coming, especially not me. I tilted my head, trying not to cry, and continued to breathe into the bag.

"I'm here. I'll wait when you're ready."

He would too. He'd been waiting for this for a while. When he'd proposed, I had told him that I'd very much like to wait. Not forever, he knew that. Just a few more months. To prepare accordingly. I wanted this day to be perfect, just like him.

My business had grown. News of my engagement to a quasi-celebrity spread, and the phones hadn't stopped ringing. Coupled with the number of fundraising galas I'd worked with Cynthia Benjamin, Bliss Events had become an overnight sensation. Our wedding date had been pushed, and pushed some more, but Levi had been patient. Then finally, when he had surprised me during my last work trip to The Maldives, I'd crossed out a date on my calendar and claimed it as our big day.

That trip did something to me.

I already had the man. I had the ring. All I had to do was choose the day to say 'I do.' And that day was today. After all the waiting, and planning, it was finally here. We made it!

But now this...

"Veronica? Sweetheart? Can you say something so that I know, we know that you're okay?" Levi tried again.

I removed the bag away from my face, stood and

pulled the bench from the door. "I'm here." I thought I heard a few sighs from the other room. "Can you send everyone out? I'd like to talk to you alone."

There were some arguments. The voices were too low for me to hear what they were saying. Levi begged, "Just a moment. A few minutes. The guests are not going anywhere. Hell, they can leave if they want to. Let me talk to her."

I heard some shuffling. Then a door shut.

"They're gone, darling. Now, please tell me what's wrong."

I unlocked the door and opened it a crack. "Don't look and don't come in. It's bad luck for the groom to see the bride before the ceremony."

He sighed deeply. "I understand. Now, can you tell me what's going on?"

I gripped the door handle. "Promise you won't freak out."

"I promise." I could hear the nervous smile in his voice.

"Okay, wait." I closed the door again, moved to the vanity and grabbed a couple of things. When I opened the door again, I held the compact mirror out and tilted it so that I could see his face. He smiled at me, wiggled his fingers and mouthed 'hi'. I needed to see his expression. "Here. Take this."

He did. He stared at it with intensity. Then his face smoothed, and all I could see was... elation. "Does this mean what I think it does?" He spoke to me through the mirror.

I nodded, and realized that he couldn't see me. "Yes," I whispered through the opening.

"We're having a baby?" Levi looked so adorable with his big-as-saucers eyes.

"Yes." In truth, I was nervous. I felt that I'd been careless.

Since our engagement and subsequently, moving in together, Levi and I had talked about having children, how many we wanted, what names we could call them, what they could possibly look like. But we hadn't talked about when. With his brother back in the picture, the burden of having to take over their international family business was off his shoulders. His vineyard had been seeing successes. And I'd been focusing on my own business. Were we ready for a child?

"Veronica, can you please come out? I'm dying to kiss you and hold you. This is the best day of my life."

"Really?" I swallowed the lump in my throat.

"Of course. How can you even ask that? We are having a baby. I'm going to be a father. We're going to be parents..." He paused and my heart stuttered. "I'm going to be a father," he said again in a lowered voice. "Please come out. Let me show you how thrilled I am."

"But it's bad luck." Weak, I know. Also, once I had taken off the dress that wouldn't zip close, all I had on were a lace bra and matching panties. Not that he hadn't seen me in anything less, but I felt ridiculous. I'd imagined telling him the news differently, with more clothing. And not before our wedding.

"Would it help if I close my eyes? I promise I'd keep them closed. Just let me hold you, my love."

I pulled the mirror away after I watched him close his eyes. Slowly, I walked out of the bathroom and stood in front of him. His hands traced my face, then my neck and shoulders, and up again to cup my chin. He lowered his head and kissed me. Sweet, sensible, full of promise.

"I love you. I love us. I love our baby." This guy got me all the time. I wrapped my arms around him and crashed my lips onto his. I let him run his hands all over my body, enjoying the goose bumps spreading on my exposed skin.

I snickered as I felt him push his hips forward. "Is that what I think it is?" I looked at him.

His eyes stayed closed the entire time. He spread his lips into a wicked grin. "Can't help it, not when you're standing before me in nothing but lace and silk. What happened to your dress?"

"It wouldn't close."

Levi shook his head. "You can wear whatever you want. It's your big day."

"It's our big day," I corrected him.

He nodded and pursed his lips. "Since our guests are already waiting, do you think we can sneak a little..." He waggled his eyebrows.

"You're incorrigible. You better get out of here so I can get dressed. I think if I suck in my stomach, the dress will fit." I led him towards the door. "Wait. Where's the test?"

He patted his jacket. "Keeping it."

"Ew, you know I peed on that."

"I don't care. I'm keeping it near my heart."

Why did I panic? Why had I thought that he'd freak

out over this? This man was perfect. My love for him grew every single day, and I had zero doubts that it would die any time soon. And with a baby on the way... it was definitely possible that I would love him more.

Before he opened the door, he tilted his head down, waiting for a kiss. I gave him what he wanted. "Let's keep this between us for now." He nodded. "I'll see you soon," I promised.

"Good. I'll be the handsome devil in the tux, front and center."

❧

THE DRESS FIT. I wondered if my panic had caused me to swell. My mother and Chase helped me put my veil on. A bunch of clicking from cameras snapped around me. Since Bliss Events was now known as one of the best wedding planning companies, a few popular wedding magazines to cover my big day had approached me. I'd chosen the best one, and they'd sent a couple of photographers over.

Alex walked in, whistling. "What a vision!" His own trusty camera was slung around his neck. He had a different effect on the women around me. Nobody was safe with his good looks and his bad-boy swagger. And with him in a tuxedo, I silently wished all the single women in the wedding good luck.

I heard a deep sigh from my right. Chase. Maybe not every female was affected the same way. She looked like a million bucks in a silver silk sheath. Her makeup was done to perfection, more pastel than kohl, and it made her look demure. My eyes flitted to her, then to Alex, through the mirror. I wondered when they would give up and surrender to what fate had planned. I couldn't think of a more perfect pairing...other than Levi and me.

Alex shot several photos alongside the magazine's photographer. Before he left, he placed a kiss on my cheek, called me beautiful and told me that his brother was one lucky man.

We descended the stairs and faced the doors that would open to the large patio where our guests and the love of my life awaited. Chase stood in front of me, clasping a bouquet, looking radiant. She turned her head and spoke in a low voice, "Not too late, Nica. My bike is right outside. I can have you in Mexico in no time." I knew she was kidding. I hoped she was kidding.

"Thanks, Chase. I think I'll stay." She shrugged, smirked, and faced forward.

Eddie ambled up to me in his gray suit. "Look at you. Such a lovely girl."

I kissed him on the cheek and hooked my hand around his arm. "Thanks for doing this, Eddie." I'd wished my father was here to walk me down the aisle. I closed my eyes remembering his big smile.

When the doors opened, I took a deep breath in, and stepped toward the man of my dreams, the love of my life, and to my future.

EPILOGUE: POUR TOUJOURS ET Á JAMAIS

LEVI

*S*he took my breath away.

As Veronica stepped into the light, I felt a familiar tug, followed by an addictive thrill in my heart. She was beautiful. The crystals on her dress caught the rays of the sun, causing an ethereal glow around her as she walked down the aisle.

The collective gasp was loud enough to hear through the fast tempo of my pulse. Even after all the times we'd been together, the sight of her turned me into something akin to an anxious teen boy gushing over his first love. But that was exactly Veronica was to me—my first, true love.

Her chest rose and fell as she breathed deeply. A blush colored her cheeks. Telltale signs that any moment now, she'd be shedding tears. I silently beckoned to her to look at me. And she did. I placed a hand on my chest. She knew what I was trying to convey—

I'm here for you. I love you. I am your strength, as much as you are mine.

We kept our gazes locked until we faced one another, and she reached for my hand, ready to take our vows.

⁂

WE RACED BACK up the aisle and into the confines of the vineyard's manor. Petals rained upon us as everyone cheered.

Moving past the patio doors, I decided to steal a moment alone with my new wife.

"Where are we going, Levi?" Veronica asked, lifting her long dress off the sleek marble floor. "We have to take pictures."

I only smiled at her before scooping her up in my arms. Ignoring, Jewel's calls, I walked into my home office, kicked the door closed with one foot, and locked it.

Bringing Veronica back down on her feet, I pressed her against the door. Her hands moved underneath my tuxedo jacket and grasped at the fabric of my shirt, when I leaned down and covered her lips with mine. I could feel the heat of her skin, and the quick tattoo of her heart against my chest. She had quite the same effect on me.

"I can't believe we're having a baby," I said against her parted lips, still swollen from my kiss.

"Me too. I'm so happy."

"Should we talk about names?"

Veronica laughed. "We can, but our wedding guests

will start to wonder. We have dinner to go through and a bit of dancing, then tonight we can talk about names."

I nipped at the soft skin on her exposed neck. "I'm sorry, sweetheart. There might not be a lot of talking going on tonight."

"There shouldn't be a lot of talking going on now," Veronica said in a hushed, silky voice.

"I'm a big fan of that idea."

"Shhh..." Veronica placed a single finger on my lips, looking at me from under her lashes. "Less talk, more kissing."

I trailed kisses over soft skin under her chin, down the column of her neck, and above the neckline of her dress, while she let my hands explore. I lifted her dress and exposed the vintage garter wrapped around one of her thighs as I raised her leg against mine.

Who was I to disappoint my wife?

⁊⁊

DINNER WAS A RELAXING AFFAIR. Veronica opted for a long table, covered with unbleached linen, rather than separate seating. We had chosen a perfect setting under a row of wooden trellises, with the abundance of grapes and leaves as our canopy. Three crystal chandeliers drooped from the arbor, which added to the charm and elegance of the variety of flowers adorning the middle of the table. Instead of traditional, individual place settings, our eight-course meal was served family style.

It was about unity. Our friends and family laughed and shared stories until the skies had darkened, and we

MICHELLE JO QUINN

returned to the large patio where the ceremony had been held. A thousand sparkling lights transformed the patio into a fairytale-like setting. The white chiavari chairs had been replaced with cocktail tables, reupholstered antique loveseats and chaise lounges, where our guests could continue to enjoy each other's company and drink wine produced in our vineyard. In the midst of the seating, our chosen soul Motown band had set up for the night.

Veronica had commissioned Jewel to take over the function. It had taken them exactly two hours to come up with the perfect reception setting. I had asked Veronica if it was difficult for her to let Jewel take over the reins, and she'd replied with a resounding 'no'.

Jake, my best man, stood in front of the mic stand as the guests mingled. "Ladies and gentlemen, please welcome Levi and Veronica for their first dance as husband and wife."

We walked hand in hand to the middle of the appropriated dance floor, and waited for the band to start playing our song. Veronica and I hadn't taken the time to sit down to choose our song, listing and playing one after the other, as other couples might have done. Rather, we'd send a message or call each other when a song played on the radio. Perhaps, it was one of the most difficult parts of the whole planning stage, considering everything else had been so easy. It had taken us a few months to find it.

I'd arrived home late one night after a trip back to France. Veronica had readily moved into the penthouse after the proposal. It had taken less than a day to have some of her belongings moved, and the rest had stayed in her apartment, since Jewel had sublet it. I'd found Veronica in the penthouse kitchen, baking cookies for a bake sale she'd volunteered for. The sound system was blasting in the background. She was covered with flour. She'd wrapped a floral apron around her waist, and there was a splotch of melted chocolate along one side of her hairline.

I'd caught her red-handed, a finger stuck in her mouth while she waited for a batch of cookies to be done. "I'm making sure this batch tastes good," she had reasoned, her lips smacking as she pulled her finger out.

The kitchen was a mess. Her eyes were round like saucers, a great ol' sign that she'd had enough sugar in her system to last her a month. I walked up to her, thinking of other ways she could spend all that energy that night. With two fingers, I swiped away the melted chocolate, and wiped it on her apron. She stuck her finger in the bowl filled with cookie dough and offered it to me. How could a man not take it?

"Sweet," I said, with a wide smile on my face, after licking the cookie dough off her finger.

"Triple chocolate cookie."

"Hmmm...I like that," I hummed in her ear. Circling my hands around her waist, bringing her hips flush against mine, I swooped down for a deep, long kiss. She tasted of decadent chocolate and desire. Veronica intertwined her fingers behind the back of my neck during that welcoming, fervent kiss.

A different song played. The ideal romantic ballad. Veronica and I inched our heads away from each other so that we could stare at one another, and both smiled. We knew that we had found the song, "Thinking Out Loud" by a soulful, young talent.

Just like that night, I took Veronica's hand in mine for our first dance, but instead of the ten-piece band starting the tune, the artist himself walked in front of the microphone, with his guitar slung around his neck. Veronica gasped at the surprise appearance.

"Did you do this?" she asked me.

I shook my head. "I wish I had." It had occurred to me to contact the singer's reps, and as much as I'd tried, I was told that he had a previous engagement. So what was he doing here on our wedding? I looked around us and spotted Alex. His focus was on his camera, but for a few seconds, he glanced up and gave me a quick nod.

"I found the culprit," I told Veronica, and cocked my head to one side.

She placed her head on my shoulder as the song began. "We'll have to send him a big thank you gift for this."

"Maybe we can send someone else to thank him." I angled us to face her maid of honor, Chase.

"I don't know, babe," she muttered in my ear, "She said she wasn't interested."

"Do you believe that?" Granted Alex and Chase hadn't been around each other much, and whenever they had been, all they'd done was argue. Yet, I'd thought I'd seen an instant chemistry when they were first introduced. "You didn't like me much when you met me."

My wife let out a small chuckle. "Yeah, but that's because you groped my ass that night."

"You remember that?"

"How could I forget? You were as handsome as the devil, and smiled like one too. It was the first time, in a long time, that I'd felt a flutter in my belly."

"You did? Why didn't you ever tell me? And you acted indifferent toward me."

"Honestly? I was terrified. Girls like me didn't get involved with boys like you."

"Ouch." I brought our intertwined hands over to my chest, feigning hurt.

"Oh, stop it. You still got the girl at the end."

I spread my lips into what she'd called a devilish grin. "That I did, darling, that I did. And I don't intend to ever let you go."

"Good," she said, bring her head back onto my shoulder. "This is where I belong...with you."

While the song continued, Veronica and I swayed with the rhythm, under the thousand miniature lights and the stars. My mind wandered to our future, with her beside me as my wife, and with her as the mother of our children.

Life could not be any better.

***

Read on for Chasing Bliss (Book 3) Excerpt

Proposing Bliss - Playlist

Can't Help Falling In Love – Haley Reinhart
See You Again, Love me Like You Do, Sugar – Megan
Davies
Hands to Myself - Barfalk
Nobody But Me – Michael Bublé
Still Falling for You – Ellie Goulding
Fais-moi Tourne Encore – Ariane Brunet
Everything – Michael Bublé
Stay with Me – Angus and Julia Stone
Crazy in Love – Daniela Andrade
Fresh Eyes – Andy Grammer
Thinking Out Loud – Ed Sheeran

ABOUT THE AUTHOR

USA Today Bestselling Author, Michelle, is addicted to romance. She believes in happily ever afters and loves writing about couples who get there.

When not writing, she props her feet up on her favorite lounger and binges on Netflix shows, or reads one or two books at the same time. She enjoys red wine, dark chocolate, cake, and can talk your ears off about delicious food. Travelling is high on her list, whether alone, with friends or family.

Michelle lives in Ontario, Canada with her husband, two amazing children and a cuddly maltese-yorkie dog named Scarlet.

DON'T MISS UPDATES ON UPCOMING WORKS, SALES OR GIVEAWAYS, SIGN UP FOR MICHELLE'S BI-WEEKLY NEWSLETTER: BIT.LY/MJQUINNNEWSLETTER

Connect with Michelle:

www.michellejoquinn.com

michellejoquinn.com

ALSO BY MICHELLE JO QUINN

www.michellejoquinn.com

THE BLISS SERIES

Planning Bliss

Proposing Bliss

Chasing Bliss

Santa Bébé (A Christmas Bliss Novelette)

Finding Bliss (Winter 2017)

WHEN HE FALLS (A New Adult Novel)

WHEN SHE SMILES (Coming 2018)

LOVE IN BLOOM (A Collection of Short Stories)

STANDALONE

THE MISTER CLAUSE (A Holiday Romance)

HARLEY (A Rockstar Romance)

WINTER'S KISS (part of IMAGINES ANTHOLOGY)

SUMMER OF BUTTERFLIES (Coming Soon)

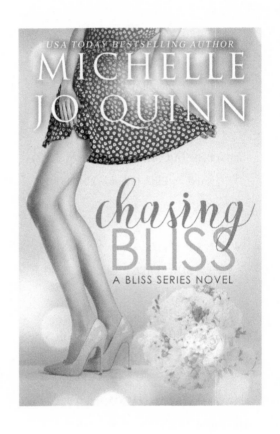

ANTECEDENT

I bent my knees and scooped up my bestie into a massive hug. Let's get something straight, I was no hugger. I had hugger-radar, and it came in handy whenever I met people who just loved to give hugs. It didn't matter if I felt like a marble statue as soon as they made contact, or that I growled like a feral lioness before they even stepped forward. Huggers were huggers. End of story.

And I'd become one.

Not being able to see Nica as soon as she'd flown in from Paris with her now-fiancé, Levi, was torturous. She'd gone through some crazy events in Paris, and I wasn't there to help her. I'd had family drama before, not that I'd ever share, but being in the middle of some other family's shitstorm wasn't any better. This woman shouldn't have gone through that alone. I'd been powerless to stop her from getting hurt. Thank the ever-loving Universe she survived and came home unscathed. And happy. And engaged!

"Chase...can't breathe," she wheezed against my leather jacket. When I released her, her face was blotchy, and she had a dent on her forehead with the same diameter as the snap of my jacket.

"Sorry...I lost my bearings for a sec." I threw her a crooked, unapologetic grin.

Nica placed a hand, one that was adorned with a huge sparkler, on her chest. "I almost suffocated between your boobs. Next time, give me a warning."

"Holy smokin', would you look at that!" I grabbed her hand. She preened and let me scrutinize the piece. "Art Deco. Nice. What year?" I'd seen the ring before, when her fiancé asked me to help out with his proposal, but on Nica, it shone even brighter.

She shrugged, a blush heating up her cheeks—the modest bride to be. "1940's. His grandfather gave it to his grandma. Isn't it sweet?"

"Sweet?" I scoffed. "I bet he got laid."

"Chase!" The red on her face intensified as we both laughed. She rolled her eyes and admitted, "Maybe just a little."

"A little? Ha!"

Nica covered her face with her hands, stifling a snort. "Okay, a lot, but not because of the ring."

"Mmm-hmm. Where's the lucky bastard now?"

I leaned my butt against her glass desk, and over my shoulder I watched Nica walk around it to rearrange the magazines and files the way she always wanted them—organized, OCD freak-style. Gotta love her for it.

Without her, our little event planning business, Bliss Events, would have burnt down to the ground even before it was set to open, and I would have turned to ashes with it. Nica had saved me. She didn't know it, and I wouldn't know how to tell her other than being loyal to her, but she had.

"He's outside, waiting for his brother to finish smoking," Nica replied as she sat down.

"The shit-disturbers are here?" I glanced over my shoulder to Nica, and scrunched my face up as though bile just filled my mouth. Two Laurents in this small office. Just what I asked for this morning—coffee, donut, and egotistical men. I'd never met the brother but I could only assume his head was as inflated as Levi's.

Nica gave me the "Chase behave yourself" look. I scowled at the window, which faced the lot, and crossed my arms over the front panels of my jacket. "Am I right or what?"

"Give them a chance." She sighed. "You know Levi's staying put. I'm not letting him go anywhere. We're getting married and that's that. And his brother Alex is not so bad once you get to know him."

I snorted, scoffed, and snorted again. "Nica, you think that about everyone." I turned around to face her, bringing my palms down on her desk. "'He's not so bad,'" I imitated, "'He's only a bit of a handful, but he's really sweet. You're going to love him. He's Levi's brother. Enough said.'" Yes, I could be a handful as well, but Nica knew I'd scale Mt Everest for her; all she had to do was ask.

"Glad you missed me too, Chase."

I heard the remark, soaked in sarcasm, behind me. Levi sauntered over to his future wife. I looked up to the flat ceiling and hoped that I wouldn't become a murder suspect today. Nica reached for one of my hands and smiled. Her fiancé (vomit) smirked at me before leaning down to give Nica a kiss (double vomit). A joke about only a mother being able to love him played on the tip of my tongue. But I caught Nica's pleading gaze, and I had to retract my fangs. For now.

Straightening up, I heaved a sigh and extended my hand. All for my best friend. "I heard congratulations are in order." We shook hands. I spread my lips into a flat smile, and muttered between my teeth, "You lucky sonofabitch." Levi dropped my hand, and I wiped mine on my jeans.

"Chase, play nice." Nica tilted her head, exasperated at my antics.

"Fine." With an eye roll, I continued, "I promise not to set your tuxedo on fire on your wedding day."

A snigger came from behind me, and I turned so fast I got whiplash. My eyes felt like they were about to pop out of their sockets. The muscles on my temple twitched.

Trouble sat on Nica's office couch, with dark, mussed, James Dean hair, and decked out in full leather. His booted feet were propped up and crossed over the dainty coffee table, which Nica and I had spent hours sanding and refinishing to perfection. And he smirked like the devil.

"Chase, meet Levi's brother, Alex," Nica piped up behind me.

I always thought life was a bitch. A bitch who loved to inconvenience me. It had been years since I'd met someone like this guy—Alex. He twirled a cigarette around his left index and middle fingers. Fingers that girls would notice. Fingers that women would clamor for a chance to lick. Fingers that undoubtedly symbolized riveting pleasures, and pure, white-hot ecstasy. Fingers of a man who had rendered me speechless.

Say something. Anything!

An almost-word gurgled from my mouth, which brought another snigger out of Trouble incarnate. He locked gazes with me as he stood, all six feet and five inches of hot-damn hotness, and stalked to where I was frozen. Instead of shaking my hand (not that I offered mine), he leaned forward and placed two swift kisses on both my cheeks. Warmth ebbed in me, blossoming from the tips of the miniature hairs on the back of my neck, and down to the little polished nails of my pinkie toes.

I wheezed, about ready to pass out, and willed myself to breathe and get a grip.

Oh, I got a grip all right. My hands, of their own traitorous volition, raised and grasped at the lapels of his leather jacket.

His blue eyes burned into my being, reached past into my retinas and captured my soul (apparently I had one, despite what others believed). His lips, full and red, quirked at one corner into a blasted, knowing smirk.

"Pleasure to meet you too, Chase." If sex was a person and spoke, it would sound like Alex—decadent and smooth with an exotic accent. The beautiful bastard ran his bottom lip between his sparkling teeth, inches from mine. My core tightened. And I knew then that he had me. Unfortunately, he knew it too.

This was so. Freaking. Inconvenient.

Life was a major bitch.

࿊

"DRINK YOUR SCOTCH AND STOP POUTING." Nica gave me her warning stare. I should tell her it made her look constipated, rather than threatening. The art of the scowl couldn't be taught. It was a skill which one mastered with practice, and which I had perfected to a tee.

I jutted my head forward, away from the back of the leather booth, slouching as I glared at my bestie. She'd invited me to have dinner with her fiancé and the brother. I could be doing better things, like color-coding my underwear drawer or refilling my non-existent spice jars. "Why am I here?" I asked.

Nica unfolded her napkin, refolded it into a freaking swan, and rearranged all her utensils. She'd chosen a fancy-pants restaurant for this lovely gathering (note the big ass hint of sarcasm there).

"To celebrate my engagement, and to talk about my wedding." She beamed at me.

I called BS. We could be talking about the wedding at work, while finishing off a couple of bottles of wine clients had given us, and a bag of chocolate eggs I'd found stashed behind one of her frilly storage boxes. Nica looked everywhere, except at me. She was a horrible liar, which made her a good person in my books.

"I could have asked Jake and Sandrine to be here too, but they're still in Paris." This girl was killing me.

I should count my lucky stars they were out of the country. Jake was Nica's ex, and Levi's best friend, and Sandrine was Jake's new wife and Levi's cousin. How messed up was that situation? And people said the world was such a big place. Puh-lease! It added to reasons why I shouldn't be here. I didn't want to have to face Alex again. Not after that embarrassing moment in Nica's office. I shuddered at the memory of him...Alexandre Laurent—such a pompous name—and the way I'd reacted to that ingratiating smirk of his as I held on to his jacket like it was a freaking life raft.

As soon as I'd realized what I'd done, I let go of him as though I'd suffered third degree burns on my hands. I'd checked them too, back and front. Alex had chuckled, low and hushed, and God help me, oh so freaking sexy. I'd made a poor excuse of having to check on something work-related and dashed out of Nica's office, *my* cheeks burning for once.

And now, we sat, Nica and I, in front of each other, waiting for Levi and Alexandre. After chugging my drink, I winced and said, "We can talk about your wedding plans at work."

She was going to ask me to do something that wouldn't bode well for me. No wonder she'd ordered me a double scotch before I arrived.

"Spit it out, Nica, or I leave." I leaned forward, crossing my arms over the white linen tablecloth.

Nica straightened in her seat, ducked her chin and peeked under her lashes. "Can you show Alex around San Francisco?"

I was about to throw my napkin down and run out when she grabbed my arm, held on with a death grip, and spoke rapidly. "Please, hear me out. Alex has never visited San Francisco, and he's here for less than a week. I feel like you'll be able to show him things that interest him. You guys are kind of the same, you know."

I sputtered out a response, "Gah... Wha... Nica? Could you insult me more?"

"I wasn't trying to insult you! Chase, please." Cue her doe-eyed look.

I was off my seat, gathering my stuff. "Why can't Levi do it?"

"Levi has to go to Napa. Alex is going there at the end of the week, and Levi has to make sure it's up to par. And before you say it, I can't, because I have a million things to take care of that piled up while I was away." I narrowed my eyes at her, and she had the audacity to pout. "Please, Chase, he's not that bad."

I shook my head, furious at my so-called bestie for putting me in such an awkward position. For once, I couldn't go with Nica's plan. Not when it meant being alone with Trouble. I could still smell his musk comingling with his leathers. It smelled like a big mistake.

Once we were alone in her office, Nica had sat me down and expanded on the situation between Levi and his brother Alex. "Alex was engaged, years ago." She fluttered her eyes and double-checked that the door was shut tightly before continuing. "The girl, Simone, cheated on him and with someone so close. Alex's initial suspicion was Levi, but he claimed innocence, even when Alex beat him to a pulp." She paused, mulling the rest of it in her head. There was more to this story than she'd wanted to share. "The fight caused a riff between the brothers, which lasted over a decade. But they're starting to patch things." I'd speculated as much. Most of the time, only two things came between brothers—money or a woman. Involving myself in this circus could cause a lot more issues than any of us would want. *No, thanks.*

Nica must have seen the determination in my eyes. She took the damned napkin again and this time, folded it into a rabbit before saying, "Okay. I thought I'd ask. Maybe Jewel will do it." She reached into her purse for her phone and typed a message, I assumed to Jewel, our friend and colleague. I hated to disappoint Nica, since she'd never disappointed me. "There. Done." Before she could slip it back in her purse, it vibrated. "That was quick! Jewel's more than happy to do it. You're off the hook."

Alex would be safe in Jewel's company. Safer than with me. I would most likely end up punching him in the gut once or twice. Jewel was a sweet girl, a little excitable at times, but she was nice and smart and pretty in that girl-next-door some guys find attractive. She was a ray of sunshine to my constant thunderstorm. And I was sure she wouldn't kick Alex out of bed if he asked for a tour of that, too. My chest constricted and my breath became ragged. Not only was I imagining one of my friends cavorting with Trouble, I was greener than Shrek because of it.

"Chase. Chase!"

Something thumped against my jacket sleeve. I caught it, looked down at my hand, saw a piece of unbuttered roll, and muttered, "What the hell?"

"What's up with you? I've been yammering here and you weren't even paying attention." Nica tore another chunk off her roll. Her gaze flitted over my right shoulder, her eyes lighting up.

Before he spoke, *I* felt him. "Well, hello again." *Alex.* I shivered despite the heat that suddenly overtook me. That voice shouldn't have been too familiar, and worse yet, it shouldn't make my knees weak. Alex and Levi stood behind Nica. Levi bent down to plant a slobbery kiss on Nica's lips, and Alex peered at me.

"Yeah, and goodbye," I snapped.

"Aren't you staying for dinner?" Alex asked.

Three pairs of eyes stared at me. Nica's were pleading. Levi seemed entertained. And Alex...well, if he'd stop licking his lips I might be able to focus on his eyes. As I dragged my gaze from his lips to his eyes, I was lost in their blue depths.

"Perfect, *après vous*." Alex waved his hand toward the booth. I imagined those hands running over my legs under the table, up my thighs and...*Stop it, Chase!*

"I have to go," I said, and rushed out of the restaurant.

When I stepped out, I welcomed the coolness of

raindrops on my face, positive there would be steam coming off me as cold rain met my heated skin. My body had warmed up under Alex's gaze. Hell, who was I kidding? My temperature spiked when I met him and had stayed that way the whole day because I did nothing but imagine him naked...with me.

"You forgot this."

I turned. There stood Alex under the eaves of the restaurant, with my helmet in his hand. His face conveyed nothing, but the fire alarm in my body screeched. Why couldn't I get hold of myself when I was near him? "Maybe one day, you could take me for a ride?"

Are. You. Kidding. Me?

Oh, I'd ride him all right.

I tried to grab my helmet but the bastard hid it behind him, so I pressed against his chest. *Breathe, Chase, breathe.* Ah hell, that was a bad idea. My heartbeat sped up when I got a good whiff of his cologne. I straightened and stepped back. "Give me my helmet." I had to raise my voice to fight against the sound of the rain.

"You've been drinking. Should you be riding?" Alex asked.

"What do you care? Give me my helmet." I sounded childish, which angered me more.

Alex shook his head, walked away from me, and headed back into the restaurant. And like a petulant child, I stomped my feet but stayed put. Hell no, I wasn't going to follow him. I trudged down the street, cursing Alex under my breath.

When he returned, he grabbed my hand, and asked, "Where is it?"

I stopped short and pulled back, remaining glued to the paved ground. "Where's what?"

"Your motorcycle. I'm taking you home," he bit back.

"No, you're not."

"Stop acting like a child and show me."

"I'm not showing you anything!"

Alexandre might have had enough, for he strong-armed me, his whole body flush against mine. He spoke in a gravelly, dark voice, which made me quiver. "You will do as I say. You'll show me where your motorbike is and tell me where you live, or I will..." His lips were inches from mine. I could almost taste his unique flavor through his breath. Even with the rain pelting us, his scent overpowered my senses.

"You'll what?" I challenged him, tilting my head up slightly so that I could read his eyes. My stomach flipped at what I saw in them. He was burning me with something I'd forgotten existed, igniting dormant desires. I felt my knees buckle, and at that moment, I was grateful he had wrapped an arm around me, or I would have collapsed to the ground. "It's around the corner." I gave in after swallowing the thick lump in my throat.

Alex let me go, but kept hold of my hand, muttering in French. We trudged through the rain until we got to my baby, my classic Harley. He swung a leg over it, while I stood aside, quirking an eyebrow.

"Do you even know how to operate this?"

"Just get on before the rain turns heavier."

It didn't matter. I was already all sorts of wet. He handed me the black helmet. I didn't bother arguing with him about not having one for himself. The ride would be short. I could've run to my place in less than half an hour, or taken a cab if I wanted, but I didn't want to leave my baby out on the street in the rain. What I wanted was something else, something I didn't understand.

I settled behind Alex, snaking my hands around his waist, and groaned as I discerned taut, muscular abs under his shirt. The Harley rumbled between my legs, and I held on tighter to Alex. I stiffened and kept distance between us. While we rode, I tapped his shoulders instead of telling him which turns to take. Somehow he understood and got us to my apartment in one piece.

Once my motorcycle was parked in the carport, I ran up the steps, jingling my keys in my hand. The problem with him driving me home was that he needed a way back. "Come on in and I'll call you a cab," I offered, avoiding eye contact.

I made a silent promise to myself not to rip his clothes off. But when I turned around he hadn't followed me up the steps.

"No need. I've got a ride back." He jerked his head to the side just as Levi stopped his car. These bastard brothers were going to hell. Why did I feel like I'd been played? "We better head back to the restaurant. Veronica's waiting all by herself." His subtlety at making me feel guilty wasn't all that subtle.

My keys dug into my palm. My teeth gritted. I didn't

risk speaking for fear I'd beg him to stay. Beg him! I did not beg. I unlocked my door and slammed it as soon as I walked in. A deep exhale came out as I sagged against the steel door. What had gotten into me?

Nica's words rang through my head: "He's here for less than a week." If I could avoid Alex and all his sexiness, I could spend the rest of my years in San Francisco unscathed and untouched. I could live with that.

MAMIHLAPINATAPAI

I managed to stay clear of Alex the first week he was in San Francisco.

Jewel took him everywhere. The first day they were due to meet, she sought me out and asked for suggestions. At first, I'd shrugged, and told her to consult the great Google. But she said she wanted things to be perfect for Alex, after all, *he* was perfect. And single. So was Jewel.

Once I tamped down that alien feeling of envy, I relented and listed spots to check out in the city. They returned to the office in the afternoon, laughing, having a ball. It turned me sour. Well, more sour than usual. Annoyed as hell, I left the office as soon as I could.

That night, sleep evaded me. While still in bed, I found myself thinking of other places *I'd* take Alex. I'd compiled a list for Jewel every night since, and each morning I'd hand it to her and warn her that the list was for her eyes only. Some of the places I'd written down were my secret, favorite parts of the city.

One in particular was The Wave Organ on the Marina, where I found myself every time I wanted to be alone. In a city as big and as populated as San Francisco, there were still places you could lose yourself. I felt like I was opening myself up to another person, someone who didn't even know I was doing it. And I wasn't talking about Jewel.

Every time Alex and Jewel returned from their outing, you would think I'd make myself scarce, like a sane person would. No, I waited for them to come back and chat about their day. Either I was in my office, with the door slightly ajar so their voices would carry, or I'd make myself leave my office and walk to the small kitchen, where they perched on the stools, looking over photos Alex had taken. Not once could I get myself to ask to check them out.

Whenever I was around Alex, there was a constant prickle on the back of my neck, like someone was burrowing into me with his eyes. Sure enough, when I'd glance over at him, he'd be staring fixedly at me, as though he'd just broken through the wall I'd built through the years, and could see *everything*.

I felt exposed.

There was a secret message written in the air. The current of desire was so thick it nearly choked me.

It was a silent game we played, to see who would surrender first. Secretly, it thrilled me and gave me something to look forward to. But the only time I'd ever make a move was in my dreams. In the light of day, I grasped at all my strength and forced myself to stay rooted in place, letting him think he would never get to me. I thought I'd won, until he left for France.

On the first night, knowing I wouldn't see him the next day, tightness bloomed in my chest. Still, I refused to admit I missed Alex.

"It's just heartburn," I lied to myself.

For the next few months, his visits were infrequent. Oftentimes, I'd hear he'd been in the States when he was already gone. But I would always know when he was around. Every fiber of my being felt him, and those heated glances had seared themselves into my mind.

Without another word or touch, I'd connected with Alex.

It scared the ever-living crap out of me.

❧

I WOULD HAVE BEEN able to ignore it if it weren't for Levi and Nica's wedding, when everything else went to shit. To say I couldn't recall how it all came about would be a complete lie. Everything began with a simple...

"Look...and tell me you don't want that."

"Want what?" I narrowed my eyes at the couple across the way.

"That. Love, marriage. What Levi and Nica have. They're so lucky." I glanced at Jewel, noting the silly, dreamy look on her face. She sighed, wrapped her arms around herself and swayed on the spot.

Jewel, much like Nica, was a hopeless romantic. They believed in crap like true love, love at first sight, and soul mates. Yadda-yadda. It was a load of Grade A turd, if anyone asked me.

And yet, my gaze slid past the newlyweds on the wooden floor, swaying to their first dance as Mister and Missus, and I spotted the Troublemaker. He'd been flush against the photographer from a wedding magazine that wanted to cover Nica's big day. He openly flirted, and they laughed, drank together, ate at the same side of the long table during dinner. Not that I'd paid much attention. I had managed to bag the interest of the only other eligible man in the wedding.

Out of fifty guests, half were women. Ninety-nine percent of the men were married, balding or gay. Since I was the Maid of Honor, I was expected to hook up with someone at the end of this. Those were the unwritten rules. Thankfully, Alex wasn't the only single man here. There was also that guy standing at the bar. If I could only remember his name.

It sounded like Jerry or Barry. Or was it James? Franklin? Franco? Shoot. No, I recalled noting that he resembled James Franco. Well, the James Franco lookalike had gotten me a drink, and he was back at the bar again, re-filling my glass. I'd drink anything to survive this night. Not that I didn't love Nica; I did. I'd give her my firstborn if she asked, or steal someone else's for her since I had no intentions of ever having a child. And admittedly—not out loud—Levi wasn't bad for her.

What tortured me was witnessing Alex and Miss Big Shot Photographer practically necking in front of all of Nica and Levi's guests. Had they no shame? I scoffed when missy pie threw her head back and laughed at whatever inane thing Alex had whispered in her ear.

James Franco lookalike slid right back in front of me, blocking my view of Alex and his...whatever-she-was, handing me a tumbler containing two shots of scotch.

Jewel gave me a questioning look when I, in the most saccharine voice I could muster said, "Thanks... darling." (I really should try and figure out what his name was). I knocked back the liquid, letting it burn down my gullet, before I grabbed James' arms, and dragged him to stand to my right. I sent a quick side-glance across the dance floor, and as soon as Alex looked our way, I pressed my lips onto James' mouth.

I felt him melting underneath me. Wait, that wasn't right... He was supposed to be getting harder, not... swooning? Was James swooning over my kiss? I inched away from his lips, and stared into his eyes. Sure enough, he had a glazed look on him.

Questions filtered in my mind. Did I even ask his name? What else was I missing? I scrutinized his features. Wait a dog-gone minute...

"How old are you?" I asked the swooning James Franco. There was something amiss.

"Seventeen. I'll be eighteen in three months," he drunkenly answered.

"Ah!" I let go of his arms, and he fell backwards.

The music ended, and the guests applauded the

newlyweds. The only people who'd paid attention to seventeen-year old James Franco and me were my friends, Jewel, Mateo and Gerard, who'd helped the little swooning boy up from the ground.

My eyes darted back to where Alex was—checked if he was still flirting and was relieved to see he'd left. However, that relief was short-lived when I spotted him a second later, guiding the photographer toward the main house. Everyone else was outside, waiting to get down to the dance floor. Alex and his twit would be alone in that big house. It didn't take a genius to posit what they'd be doing there, possibly in one of the bedrooms or bathrooms, all by themselves.

"Chase, what's wrong with you?" Jewel lightly slapped my arm.

I growled at her, but my wrath had no effect on Jewel. She knew me too well. "Did you see what you did to the poor boy? I thought he was gonna piss his pants." She nudged her chin toward the young— too-young— James Franco, being consoled by Mateo and Gerard. Were those tears I saw in his eyes?

I should go apologize, but what I said instead was, "He shouldn't be drinking anyway. He's underage."

"You just kissed him." Jewel propped a hand on her hip. "And he wasn't drinking. He's had juice all night."

"I—" *wasn't thinking. I was jealous. I was trying to prove a point to someone who didn't even notice me* "—need another drink." I headed to the bar and ordered a drink, which easily turned into more than one. I downed each one quickly, trying to drown the green-eyed monster in my gut.

Jewel was right to ask what was wrong with me. Ever since Trouble with the capital 'A' walked—no, freaking strutted—into my life, I'd had nothing else to think about but him.

§

NICA HADN'T SAID a word to me prior to her wedding, even though I knew she knew. Best friend vibes.

Whatever occurred inside the house with the photographer happened fast, embarrassingly fast. I sniggered internally, but only to quell my jealousy. Alex emerged with the photographer, laughing, their arms hooked together. As soon as they hit the dance floor, Alex let her go and danced with Nica, Nica's mom, Lily, and her sister, Maggie. And practically every woman after that. He even pulled one of the hired servers to the floor. I watched it all from the safety of my almost drunken stupor.

"You need to ease on the booze, girl. I can hear your liver screaming for mercy," Gerard, ever the drama queen, told me with the flamboyance of a showgirl.

He and Mateo decided to take a break from dancing and hydrate, joining me by the bar. Mateo peeled the wineglass from my grasp and exchanged it with a bottled water. "Drink this. Did you even eat anything at dinner?"

"Yes, *Mom*, I did." I rolled my eyes at Mateo, but uncapped the bottle and took a sip of the water. Truthfully, I couldn't remember the last time I'd gotten this drunk. I hoped not to turn into one of those blubbery women I'd seen in the weddings I'd been to.

Gerard cleared his throat, taking my mind off my unfinished thoughts. "Drink up, bitch." He pushed the water to my lips, and it trickled down my neck.

"What the hell, G?" I'd just grabbed cocktail napkins off the bar and dabbed at the cool liquid when I felt it— the prickle. I looked up to Gerard and Mateo, who were staring and smiling at something past my shoulder. I decided to wait and not turn.

"Fancy a dance?"

Breathe, Chase, breathe.

It shouldn't have mattered that his voice could cause my stomach muscles to tighten, or the neurons in my brain to cease all synapses. But it did.

My eyes widened, and I continued to stare at Gerard as he twirled his finger, signaling for me to turn around. *No freaking way!* But I did, because Alex was behind me, and my body—the traitor—did everything it could to get closer to him, without my permission.

The first thing I noticed up close was how he filled out the suit he wore. For a globetrotting photographer, he had a body I could stare at...not that I would. Never... I didn't have to. When it came to Alex, I was hyper aware of everything about him. I knew if I flipped his right arm over and pulled up his sleeve, I'd see a script-like tattoo, which ran from his wrist to his inner elbow. If I took another step, I'd smell leather and mint and not the suffocating scent of cigarettes.

But none of it mattered. He wasn't good for me, no matter what my brain tried to make me believe.

You're no good for him.

"What?" I asked, schooling my face to something neutral—and that was a challenge all on its own.

Alex *freaking* smirked and brushed his dark hair with a hand. "I've danced with just about every woman here..."

"And me," Gerard butted in. I cocked my head to the side and sent him a warning glare.

"Yes, and you. Excellent moves." Alex's teeth sparkled. *Flirt.*

"Thanks. You too." Gerard was outright flirting back. I'd be worried if I didn't know Alex was as straight as, well...Levi. Wait, no! I wasn't worried. Gerard was married, and his husband was snickering away behind me.

Alex returned his focus to me, and continued, "Well, as I was saying, I've partnered up with everyone that counted, except you, Chase."

"No."

Gerard gasped, and I sneered at him when I turned, showing Alex the back of my head. I gulped down the water and reached for my wine.

Alex did not relent. "C'mon. You're the maid of honor. I'm the groom's brother. We have to dance at least once."

Without looking back, I replied, "I said no. I don't dance." *Breathe, sip some wine, swallow it down, and push all the jitters away.*

"Everyone dances," Alex retorted.

Gerard nodded. "Mmm-hmmm. Everyone."

"Shut it, G," I muttered under my breath, and then

the little hairs on my arms stood as Alex closed in. I could feel the heat of his skin. I could smell that intoxicating scent.

And felt his hot breath on my ear. "One dance. One song. One hand."

What the snit? "One hand?" Now, I was curious. "What do you mean one hand?"

Alex was so close to me that the vibrations of his voice trembled against my coal-hot skin. "Dance with me and I'll only keep one hand on you at all times."

I scoffed. *No way!*

"This I have to see!" It was Gerard who said it. I sent him another warning glare but he pouted, and mouthed, *you owe me.*

Eff-to-the-uck. He got me there. Gerard and I had been friends for so long and the number of favors I'd asked from him all these years had piled on. He'd never asked for his markers, and this shouldn't even count. But I knew it did. And if I didn't agree to a dance with Alex, Gerard would make me suffer. I begged Mateo silently, but he just smiled and half-shrugged.

I knocked back the wine I had in hand, and agreed, "Fine. One dance, one song, one hand." I pointed a finger, bared my fangs at Alex, and narrowed my eyes at him. "If even a single digit of your other hand twitches my way, it's over."

Alex widened his lips, from ear to ear. He was enjoying this, the jerk. I made a note to step on his feet every chance I got. He offered a hand to me, and with a bit more hesitation, I took it. While we made our way to the dance floor, my hands shook. I caught sight of Nica with Levi talking to some guests. They looked at us with shameless smiles.

I remembered watching the two of them dance at Jake and Sandrine's wedding. They could have set the entire tent on fire, the way they moved together. Of course, it was the night that had changed everything for them, and in a way, for me.

I'd never been a fan of change. I was comfortable with my life.

Once we were on the floor, the big band switched from a fast beat to a slow ballad. Alex turned to face me, but I kept my gaze lowered. In my five-inch heels, we were almost the same height. Alex snaked his right hand around my waist, kept his left hand behind his back, and we swayed. I didn't recognize the song—it was in French—but Alex knew it by heart. And while he moved he sang it to me, his stubbly cheek pressed against mine. With a light grip on my waist, he tugged me closer, placed one of his legs between mine, and led me gliding around the floor.

I closed my eyes as his fingers whispered over my bare back, tickling the nerve endings along my spine. My heart was beating wildly by the time his hand left my lower back and stroked up the side of my ribs and down along the length of my arm. With a flick of his hand, he raised my hand up and ghosted his knuckles along the outside of my arm. Then he clasped my hand and somehow, made me twirl.

This man was like a drug. He'd invaded my senses and woke up dormant feelings. My body hummed and zinged. I felt alive. And I didn't like it one bit.

Somehow I was able to talk, but I kept my eyes closed. "Had a good time with the photographer?" If I could take it back, I would, though only because I sounded jealous.

Alex chuckled in my ear. "So you were watching."

"I wasn't," I lied. "But it was hard not to notice."

His chest rose with a deep inhale, and with an exhale, he said, "I showed her a few of my photographs."

"I guess it didn't impress her, since you guys were there less than five minutes."

He blew a frustrated breath in my ear. "You don't think I can give anyone pleasure in that short of a time?"

I screwed my eyes tighter when he flicked my hand again, and I turned. "I wasn't talking about…"

His hand returned to the small of my back, and he stopped. The song was done. How long it had really taken was unclear to me. My exhale was shaky once I opened my eyes, and saw no one else but him. Everything else around us was a blur.

When Alex had danced with other women, after every song ended, he'd lifted each woman's hand and kissed the back of her fingers. Waiting for him to step back and do the same with me secretly thrilled me. Except he didn't do that.

Instead, Alex's intense gaze burrowed into mine for what seemed like eternity. He leaned in and whispered, "The guesthouse in fifteen minutes, and I'll show you how much pleasure I can give a woman." Then he stepped back and walked away, leaving me trembling in my Louboutins and gasping for more air.

***

Want to Read More? Chasing Bliss is available in ebook and paperback formats.

www.michellejoquinn.com

EVERYTHING SHE EVER WANTED

A NOVEL BY LIZ DURANO

I was never into fairy tales.

BUT DISCOVERING a real live princess in my house reminds me of the story of the three bears and some chick who breaks into their pad, eats all their food, and sleeps in their beds.

Just like the one that's in mine right now.

At first, I thought she was dead, but the rise and fall of her chest told me that she was just passed out, probably from the half-empty bottle of Bordeaux I'd been saving for a special occasion. Two grand down the drain, courtesy of Goldi-effing-locks here, who's not only passed out cold, but she's also naked.

I should walk out right now and let her be...

But I can't. Not when there's something else next to

the Bordeaux, something that shouldn't be here. And it's sitting on top of a note that begins with the words...

"I'm sorry I failed you..."

http://WWW.LIZDURANO.COM